LAST YEAR AT BETTY AND BOB'S

A NOVELTY

Before you start to read this book, take this moment to think about making a donation to punctum books, an independent non-profit press

@ https://punctumbooks.com/support

If you're reading the e-book, you can click on the image below to go directly to our donations site. Any amount, no matter the size, is appreciated and will help us to keep our ship of fools afloat. Contributions from dedicated readers will also help us to keep our commons open and to cultivate new work that can't find a welcoming port elsewhere. Our adventure is not possible without your support.

Vive la Open Access.

Fig. 1. Hieronymus Bosch, *Ship of Fools* (1490–1500)

First edition published in 2017 by Open Humanities Press.
Second edition published in 2018 by 3Ecologies Books/Immediations, an imprint of punctum books.
https://punctumbooks.com

ISBN-13: 978-1-947447-79-0 (print)
ISBN-13: 978-1-947447-80-6 (ePDF)

LCCN: 2018953766
Library of Congress Cataloging Data is available from the Library of Congress

Book design: Vincent W.J. van Gerven Oei

HIC SVNT MONSTRA

LAST YEAR AT BETTY AND BOB'S
A Novelty

Sher Doruff

Contents

Every bit of blue is precocious.

Gertrude Stein, *Tender Buttons*

You say to the boy open your eyes
When he opens his eyes and sees the light
You make him cry out.
Saying O Blue come forth
O Blue arise
O Blue ascend
O Blue come in
[...]
Blue protects white from innocence
Blue drags black with it Blue is darkness made visible
Blue protects white from innocence
Blue drags black with it
Blue is darkness made visible

Derek Jarman, *Blue*

Acknowledgments

Thanks to Karen Dunn and Lucy Cotter for their sharp, tenacious editing assistance. To Erin Manning and the Senselab for their enduring support, and to Andrew Stapleton for his help in preparing the manuscript.

To all and every germ of idea and sensation spread by artists, thinkers, students, colleagues, friends, family, neighbors, media, and spam folded into the pages here.

Foreword

Day 222

This is all so fucking tedious.

Day 223

I requested a new journal today, oversized with unlined pages. The cute intern with snakey dreads delivered it within an hour, taking the trouble to buy one from an art supply store so the paper quality is heavier and better suited for ink, markers, and glue. One-hundred and eighty gsm. I figured the lack of structure would free me from a linear left-to-right inclination. I feel like drawing and pasting feral collages with images from the net and my phone. They let me use the wifi printer at the reception desk. I'm sure it annoys the hell out of them. I can't quit myself entirely from words just yet. Each passing day the responsibility to leave some kind of trace in my own hand confronts me. The shape of my thoughts surprises as they squirt from my pen. I try to write in my mother tongue, avoiding the inflections of this new language as much as possible.

Day 224

I feel my capacity to embrace change will soon exhaust itself. I'm fast approaching the threshold of too much, though differentiating my past from what I am becoming is no longer fraught with angst. Clock time is an abstraction. Sleep doesn't save me from anything. A storm rages inside and outside the boundaries of my skin, my hair, my tongue. Oddly, what I most miss of my recent past is the Purello ritual. Doomed to a singular reality, weirdly surreal that it is, I have lost all sense of an exit, an escape hole. I sit here, encased in the discomfort of an antiseptic cork-lined room in the quarantine wing of an epidemiology clinic somewhere mountainous. It looks like Zurich outside the porthole window. I try to imagine I'm Marcel Proust rather than a lab specimen but I can't shake the residual image of Man Ray's death photo of the guy. The "Team" have kindly brought in a few pieces of my own furniture to upgrade the comfort factor but, to be honest, these objects only heighten my dis-ease. The fancy new treadmill is a non-replacement for walks in the park. I refuse to pursue the obvious analogy any further. Within the constrained cubic dimensions of this germ-free space I'm sprouting phobias. Claustrophobia, androphobia, cynophobia, the list is endless. Happily, my tendency towards neophobia is overwhelmed by the rapid rate of change itself. Change is the new stasis. I want to run wild and feel distance and proximity shift around me, watch objects grow from peas to planets in scale. I remain in position XYZ. Everything stays the same size while moving.

Day 227

Daytime TV is a disaster.

Day 245

*They prick me so often I'm covered with needle marks on every limb, the membrane of my very tough skin surface a moonscape of purples and blues. Though I'm in no pain whatsoever I get a daily hit of morphine, compensation I suppose for the absence of my preferred altering substance. Perhaps they wish to keep me in a suspended state of dependency? It's a power play, for sure, "We must keep the beast at bay," but I'm up for the game. What do they call it in American football? A Hail Mary pass? That's **their** play. Anyway, I have to admit this drug has a pleasant kick and it's about all I have to look forward to as the days go by aside from ruminating on the ever-so tiresome constant of transformation. Hopefully cathartic events documented in this journal will help deflect my meaner mood swings. We're all counting on that. I think they're secretly afraid to make me angry. They tiptoe very carefully around my dispositions which of course are perfectly visible on my cheek. Sometimes I flash a fiery blinking red which translates to "max threat" on their scale but it's a "horniness alert" on mine. I haven't told them the truth of it because I enjoy watching the fear level increase on their faces. It keeps my boredom at bay.*

1

An Occurrence

Once inside the enormous edifice dedicated to the last gasp of an anachronistic trade, she slipped. Here she was again in the PostOffice. The reflective surfaces in this curved glass and polished brass monument deflected any illusion of service. She thought the building had a mutant feel to it, the errant progeny of a science museum and a Trump hotel.

She was well aware of the urban myth swelling from the aura of the long west wing of this structure. She ambled to the notorious sector on the fifth level in no rush. The rush was to come. For once there, where gilded public storage lockers marked a repetitive landscape of forgotten matters, lay a nearly frictionless floor, slicker than a freshly Zambonied ice hockey rink. She'd heard this place was commissioned as a quasi-functional architectural art/science proposition. She doubted this. There was no plaque, no curatorial legend, no explanatory handout. This place was a well of Chinese whispers, minimal, fluorescently lit and slick slick.

The swish hallway allowed visitors and patrons unusual transport opportunities. Once a nuanced push-off technique had been mastered, super-gliding in everyday street shoes was on offer. Though the speed one could attain on this rarified surface was initially alarming, dangerous even, many returned to repeat the thrill. Starting and stopping a skid with pinpoint accuracy required a technique that came quickly to skiers and skaters. Few PostOffice visitors had yet to competently achieve it. Accidents were rife during peak hours.

She'd been here once before, managing a few tentative skids. Today, though dressed in bulky everyday winter wear totally inappropriate for athletic activity, she'd spontaneously veered from her early morning routine into the imposing building. She fancied a full-fledged fling at the POMOC, the infamous PostOffice MotionCorridor, so dubbed by zeitgeist skidders. Her timing was opportune. The place was dull quiet.

Eyes closed, she mentally fast-forwarded the "How to Skid for Beginners" *YouTube* clip. The flashy moonwalk technique was cool oh and yeah the warrior pose was trending but stick with the basics she told herself.

Bette B scanned the walls and handrails for anchors to slow an accelerating slide. Assaying a number of safety islands and handholds she assumed the take-off posture. Timidly she exerted a kind of push, and felt tingle of corporeal effort. Then she was off!

On her first skid she attained a ±20 kph pace but botched the stop. Unable to stay on her feet her butt hit the tarmac hard. Well-padded, no black and bluing welt would likely erupt. Trying again, she wobbled on the push-off but remained upright and in partial control of her momentum. By her third attempt she was poised and ready for a full run and whizzed down the long hall in a state of delighted, adrenaline panic. Thirty kph? Forty? Flash memories of her first ride on the Stratosphere roller coaster blew through the rush of her pulsing blood.

The pinpoint stop, her first ever, told her to quit while she was ahead. For a moment she wished there'd been a witness, an audience to her achievement. Overcome by an endorphin cocktail of exhilaration and exhaustion she'd had enough for one day.

Step by slippery step, she carefully plodded her way from the friction-free hallway back to the central rotunda. She focused on her soles swiping the floor. Occasionally she glanced up to catch locational bearings. It was then she noticed what had always been there. Near the halfway point a tiny brownish figure was rocking gently as if to a beat. Squinting at first, then eyes wide, she apprehended a lone animal of the type often seen dining on the subway tracks far below.

Even from a distance she could make out that the claws of its rodent feet, like her own leather-soled pumps, were incapable of firmly gripping the gleaming synthetic veneer of the tarmac. Skidding, the animal began to speed directly towards her. For a nanosecond she was amused, expecting it to slip by as one passing on a parallel runway. Instead, it was heading straight for her bare naked legs. She froze. Before she could gulp another packet of air into her lungs, the animal had ascended the length of her coat and, having reached the vertical limit, pressed its snout against her left cheek. Its whiskers pricked against her nostrils. She did not, could not, exhale.

Perhaps her startled body over-exaggerated the import of the event but it felt like a life-or-death moment. What confused disorientation the rodent may have felt she couldn't know. As in films, her perception was in slo-mo though the speed of the gesture with which she squeezed the animal's snout in her right hand to incapacitate its mouth as a biting machine was impressive. She could feel the solid mass of its long incisors as she pressed its jaws closed. The danger momentarily abated, terror flushed through her organs and limbs as she let out the air from her lungs. She didn't yet know it had scratched her face in its own survival throes. Adrenaline suspended any sensation of pain. Pushing her thumb into its windpipe, she cut off its flow of oxygen until its heavy body fell limp in her hands. The sheep wool of her mitten covered its eyes so they had no intimate contact during this exchange.

She then dropped this thing as one would a hot potato. Lying in the middle of the glassy floor she sensed it was in a semi-conscious state and might recover its bearings at any moment, scampering again up her leg in retribution or fear. She looked around for help, for guidance of some kind.

The corridor was still unpeopled save for a thickset older couple dressed in layers of heavy clothing. Carefully pushing a cart with several stacked suitcases and plastic wrapped cardboard boxes from a mini-storage company, they cautiously approached, affirming without words the many implications of Bette B's plight in the unfolding situation.

In her mind's eye, a circular tracking shot followed, panning the composition of the scene: a comatose rodent on a shiny, super-synthetic floor, her wooly traumatized self, a stoic elderly couple in matching, oversized blue coats heaving a metal luggage cart. Huddled together, all are speechless.

Bette B had experienced a fleeting visual perception, evoked in the hysterical microsecond of disabling an animal's breathing apparatus, of a surprisingly fluffy under neck fur. In a flash of dubious recognition, the metro rat appeared as a long-haired, short-snouted guinea pig or gerbil. A species of the cuddly domesticated variety adored by *Homo sapiens*. In that flickering, the animal became a non-threatening other and she Goliath to its puny David, a statuesque tower of organic comfort in the speedy-slick, unearthly wormhole that was the POMOC.

Just how an ethical instant emerges from an event's unfolding is a question she's been probing for some time with little success. Speculative armchair-style tinkering leaves her unsatisfied just as the full flush of sensuous experience overwhelms any juridical balancing act. Generally, she runs away, fast, from philosophical discussions of moral coding. Now she feels there's nowhere to hide, no escape hole.

Presumably, the inert body of the animal will be dealt with in some fashion by someone; clubbed to a certain death by a PostOffice custodian and unceremoniously incinerated. This is its likely fate. It may be handed to a lab for preemptive bacterial analysis or bagged and carted off to a university biology class for dissection as city vermin have recently been categorically upgraded as fair trade research specimens. Or perhaps, as happens in fairy tales and crime thrillers, she is an unwitting protagonist in the tendrils of the rodent's storyline. In the event's ethical nanosecond, this is what she imagined as she rendered the potentially toxic animal flaccid. In any case, this is the story she tells herself, walking home at an everyday pace along the resistant, concrete footpaths of an urban conclave buzzing with imperceptible forces affecting every move she makes.

2

Bette B

Her nerves were frayed. An animal a fraction her size and doubtless twice as fearful had prompted a survival response she can't yet explain. She saw, or thought she saw, felt or thought she felt, her life in the balance of an action. The swift advance of chance was coupled to reactive anxiety in an interspecies encounter. She, Bette B, had proved victorious in a spontaneous duel in which an enemy had not declared itself as such. She may well have disposed an innocent, entangled in its own reptilian fight, flight, or freeze survival catharsis.

Leaving the scene of the crime before any authority had yet responded, she was dazed, needing the reassurance of normalcy her home would afford. Having thanked the blue-coated couple for their attention, all three had carefully stepped along their ways. The rat or guinea pig, breathing shallowly in the middle of the POMOC, would, yes or no, regain its composure and slip away, finding a hole through the gleaming façade to its netherworld as rodents do. Or it would perish there.

At home in her apartment, situated on a relatively quiet residential street just off a shopping artery, she was able to mix herself a gin and tonic, put the scratchy Miles

Kind of Blue LP on the player and collapse into her favorite reading chair to remember what had occurred.

Nerves settling, she walked to her bathroom in which hung the only mirror in her apartment. She examined her face and neck, finding a small four-stroke scratch on the jawbone of her left cheek. In a rush as palpable as the initial "attack," she felt fear move from her gut to her throat, choking her gasp.

Talking to herself she mapped the possibilities.

"Uhh, uhh, a biopower morality play maybe ... or Christ, another mythic animal story." Her imagination often took her on wild rides even in the most unremarkable of situations. Faced with the immediacy of real-life drama, she felt a latent pang for cosmic adventures, drifting weightlessly, blissfully, on a blanket of stardust amidst a sparkling multiverse of quasars, supermassive black holes, and bursting supernovae. Carl Sagan's spaceship. She long ago purchased her ticket to ride to the cosmic "out there." How had she been so suddenly transported to its inverse "in there"? She held her panic at bay, closing her eyes as she scaled, travelled down to the invisible realm of the quantum register. She let its equivocal mystery soothe her for a moment.

Opening her eyes to the lurid fluorescent light in this her two-meter-square water closet, she understood her new reality was oscillating somewhere between infinities of vast and vast. The messy, earthy microscopic dimension of squiggly life-form activity had never before tickled her conceptual terrain. Sure, she'd followed the rhetoric of the anthropocene with interest but her pop-sci preferences erred towards physics rather than biology. Uncomfortable with allegories outside the extremes of the infinite macro or infinitesimal micro, she took another long look in the mirror.

Squeamish. She was fucking squeamish.

3

B⊘B

He'd been wondering lately about processes of transformation. How a singular force effects another force to become something other than it is while still retaining something of what it was. It's been on his mind for some time now, often percolating with white heat while he's dropping a trail of pellet shit. He relishes a good conundrum. Loves diving into ontological problematics.

Dusk is his favorite time of day. Rubbing the residue of sleep from his eyes, he enjoys the swathe of energy a fresh evening brings. The daily tasks entailed in foraging for food and drink, on average, produce little by way of the remarkable. Edible substances are plentiful in his neighborhood. Water, of wildly variable quality, is everywhere. Male competitors, sexual partners and his exponentially expanding family move about the shared terrain amicably for the most part. The life business of survival that fully occupies so many of his species, and from what he can tell, most other species he's encountered, long ago hit a stride of patterned routine. There are dips and peaks of course, and who wouldn't look forward to daily anomalies, but generally, his existence flows with little resistance. After all, his species are renowned neophobes, preferring constancy to surprise. He's playing his part, his ecological role as a garbage man. He's calculated that in plus/minus two dozen full moons he'll be attending to a metamorphic dynamic he's witnessed thousands of times as his rigid lifeless body particulates to a dusty substance and blows away. But, and this is typical of him, he's certainly romanticized this final event.

He finds time in his waking hours, just as darkness softly descends on his field of play, to ponder just this, his field of play. He wonders if he's unusual in this? He hasn't really bonded with other rats in his 'hood and suspects they don't take their pleasures in dusk-dreaming as he does. Rather, they tend towards the pre-dawn hours for frequent, gratuitous moments of abandoned hedonism, reproductive booty calls and head counting the small ones still in the nest. He's different. He knows he's not the social beast he's meant to be. He tends towards the shamanic dividual, relishing solitary investigative adventures. The urgency of the hourly mating ritual has long since dissipated. Though not exactly celibate, he's become a lapsed breeder. He might have been ostracized by his tribe long ago were it not for his gift of an acrobatic voice laced with tonal timbres of the dawn itself. On special occasions he rivets hoards of his folk, stilling them in their scampering tracks. Enjoying celebrity status in his community he rarely abuses the privilege it brings him though he does take advantage of the latitude his clan grants him regarding his monkish temperament. As long as he puts out, sharing his beautifully resonant, exquisitely articulated song, all is right in the burrows of the rodent world that sprawls beneath the fundaments of the PostOffice.

He goes by no proper name amongst his fellows. In the democracy that is ratdom, individuals are not distinguished by characteristic labels. Identity profiling is unknown to the hoard, an attitude totally off their radar. They sense differencing as the movement of change in one from another one, and parse that very process into information. Their acute noses distill the scent of genealogy, of tendencies, of potential affirmations and negations, of lusting and desperation, of satisfaction and hunger, of warmth and chill. This is quite enough data for any rat to apprehend.

In his rarified case of celebrity, there is something else at play, additional bits of information that single him out even as he silently goes about his daily foraging business. It's as though he bares an enigmatic sign, clearly decipherable by his fellows, that reads:

It was there a horse soon dancing

His folk have come to depend on his sonic exertions when and where it matters. Their expectation weighs heavily upon him. Rather than awarding him the obnoxious levity of entitlement, it has driven him, surreptitiously, to drink.

He's not sure when his taste for fermented liquids first took hold as his feeling for time doesn't necessarily unfold chronologically. It's rather more spatial, his sensation of becoming. He feels a warp and weft between temporality and place that shifts like a dimpling surface around *felt* events and their location in the block of mattering that is his universe. He gravitates in his daily doings towards these seductive manifolds, as much for their familiarity as their strangeness. One such attractor of unparalleled magnetism is the slippery corridor in the Upper World complex. Its strange, even a tad perverse. It's home to what he calls the "Path."

An obscure tunnel, gnawed into existence by a deceased brother, winds its way to a hole, his Hole, opening to a storage room near the rotunda of this vast terrain. In this relatively tiny closet, uniformed humans, charged to keep the surface of the Path slick and smooth, store ample supplies such as:

buckets
mops
brooms
bins
wipes
hand towels
detergents
waxes
polishes
plastic gloves
squeegees.

And solvents:

hexane
turpentine
acetone
ethanol.

The last item is noteworthy. Ethanol, or as it goes by its commercial name, Spiritus, is a 94% alcoholic liquid primarily used by the uniforms to remove sticky substances from walls, floor, and handrail surfaces. It's a major task in their routine repertoire as young humans are most likely to frequent the Path leaving DNA filled saliva traces in colorful wads of butadiene-based synthetic rubber, a.k.a. chewing gum, under the protective handrails and brushed brassy benches. Though this commercial substance evaporates quickly, copious amounts spilled on the floors of the passageway on a daily basis could, in principle, effectively intoxicate or even annihilate the entire local populace of nearly any living species.

He is one of the few of his clan that venture to this well-scrubbed, food-free area. Its lures simply overpower him; strong Outside forces mesh with his inner tendencies. When he first discovered the delights of inebriation conflated with the thrill of frictionless motion he was a mere youth, exploring unknown territory. He could find no good reason to resist the perpetual, seductive call of ungodly speed and chemically induced fearlessness. He returned often to suck up the potency of the surfaces here, absorbing pure alcohol from the Spiritus residue as well as gleaning tiny dosages from the sugary, beer-tainted Bazooka that adolescent skidders leave behind.

Now a mature rodent, his lack of resistance to these pleasures feels like addiction, one he has no immediate intention of shaking. As he ages, however, he can feel a tingle of dread infecting his thrill seeking. An uneasy reticence bordering on fear now accompanies his zoom-rides as he struggles to keep his once unfaltering balance when he hits max speed. A steadily creeping mortality moves through his limbs, his organs, his spirit, with every step, with every skid he takes.

During each phase of the new and full moon, he runs into a cousin by his father's umteenth mate who chooses to be "in her cups" on a twice-monthly basis. She, this darling cousin, usually finds all the ethanol drippings she can handle in the storage closet and stations herself there. She's dead afraid to venture unto the Path itself having heard, as all rats have, haunting stories of untimely death and unfathomable disappearance from this sector. She preempts any possibility for falling prey to its coercive mysteries.

When he first encountered her in a stupor state, snuggled into a noxious rag on a storage shelf, he felt his privacy in this immense place intruded upon. Pissed off, he resisted, descending into the juvenile spraying routine of the cat species. He'd rather territorialize this area with emissions of vocal skill. But his cousin was unintimidated by his celebrity and monastic lifestyle, sneaking biweekly inside his domain. Initially irritated, he'd grown to cherish these regular social interludes with her, primarily because they would both shirk their familial reserve and let loose together. An inherited vocal gift from their father's side of the gene pool, her tipsy lower register mixes perfectly with his flamboyant high frequency oscillations though she lacks the aesthetic complexity of his tonal palette and range. They joke, with every lunar-pull cocktail, that they're rehearsing for a duet moment at his next public airing. They both know this is a polite civility. Isolated in the storage room from the tempting reverberance of the Path's acoustics, they have garnered no audience. He's content with that. She has no use for fame.

His ethanol addiction is more progressed than his cousin's. Though not given to drunkenness, he imbibes on a daily basis. A self-described "licker," exercising his tongue routinely to maintain the flexible, muscular quality of his vocal expression is a significant technique of his artisanal practice. Riding the Path exerts a complex twofold high:

1. adrenaline upper of fluid excitation
2. intoxicated downer of muscular relaxation

Skidding stimulation therefore tweaks his potential, pushes his buttons. Licking, he's aware, is an excuse for dulling his existential dilemmas even as his sensorial operandi explode.

Convinced that the licking and skidding combo helps to maintain the youthful, vibrational elasticity of his vocal folds, he vainly persists. Should he holiday from singing for some length of time, he's certain he'd feel the loss of articulating tension. His flaps would go all lethargic, corrupting the pure sonication of his output. He fears he's susceptible to laryngeal decay as he advances towards his demise. Any injury impeding his production of absurdly high frequencies massaged to magnificent effect would be devastating. The vibratory membranes and ventricular folds that surround the black hole of his tracheal tube are the tools with which he negotiates microtonal glissandi and subdued melismatic flourish. His practiced vibrato is his very own event horizon, nourishing the dark suck of his inhale.

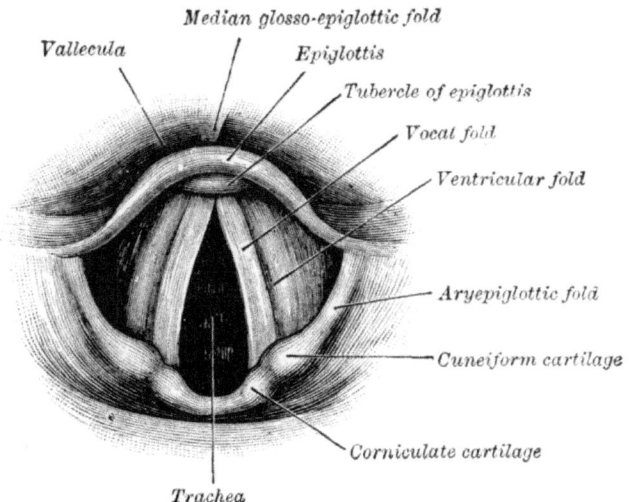

4

They

Since the POMOC episode Bette B's been adjusting to an onslaught of sudden, thankfully brief, hallucinatory episodes. In an eye blink, worlds appear replete with detailed scenarios much like the rapid onset of a dreamscape. She's convinced she is wide awake and participating in the everyday physical world catalyzing her central nervous system. But these occasional "fits" knot a curious mix of sensory and hallucinatory perceptions. She records these happenings in her notepad according to their perceived normalcy or exaggerated abnormalcy:

— The air feels damp against my skin and smells of rotting organic matter as I pass a trash container.

☑ normal

— The pulse of a jackhammer pounds the pavement somewhere near enough that its reverberation tickles my feet on the sidewalk.

☑ normal

— The vegetable shop I'm browsing, unleashes a blinding cascade of color in its tomatoes, peppers, eggplants, endive, bananas, oranges, kiwis, pecans, potted basil...

☑ normal

— The avocados in the same shop are a patented International Klein Blue (IKB).

☒☑ abnormal

— The rain drains in the street amplify Merzbow's Animal Magnetism album.

☒☑ abnormal

— A figure in a white bunny suit with ridiculously long ears hands out flyers for the opening of new fitness center.

☑☑ normal ☒ uncertain????

Hyperaware of every prick of sensation, she feels an excess of experience. Of course these kinds of scenes also play out every evening as she sleeps, if she sleeps, as she dreams, if she dreams, but her experience of the world the past few days is different somehow. She can only describe it as hallucinatory, having no other immediate vocabulary for the startling disjunction between how she thinks she feels and how she feels she thinks. There is a pervasive lucid quality to her phase shifting, a heightened state of attention.

The rat scratch on her left cheek has changed color. Initially a pinkish scrape, the four distinct claw marks swelled a bit then turned a rusty brownish hue. It appears to be healing, the tetanus shot, an RBF (rat bite fever) deterrent, doing its work behind the scenes, stultifying any bad bacterial behavior. But she's suspicious and can't shake an incipient morpho feeling, a queasy sense of alteration. But then she has always nursed an active imagination, generously nourished by a literary appetite. That reminds her...

"ONE MORNING, AS GREGOR SAMSA WAS WAKING UP FROM ANXIOUS DREAMS, HE DISCOVERED THAT IN BED HE HAD BEEN CHANGED INTO A MONSTROUS VERMINOUS BUG."

Pulling a gnarled copy of Kafka stories from the shelf, she finds what she's looking for:

Never one of her favorite yarns, her girlish squeamishness towards insects trumped any real sympathy she could drum up for the hapless Gregor. Her lack of cockroach compassion provoked confrontational ethical problems for her as for the unfortunate Samsa family. Unmitigated animality. This is a something she had not yet experienced.

Anxiously, she went about her routines, fearful as one might be of a lump in the breast or a darkening mole. Waiting for the advent of a new state of affairs, just outside the reach of one's control, she assessed the condition of her disquiet. She had the feeling that apprehensive expectation of emergence is an activity dosed with a significant degree of pathos. She then reassessed, thinking of the CERN physicists patiently and successfully anticipating the trace of the Higgs boson; astrophysicists keenly awaiting the spectacle of the Milky Way black hole feasting on its gaseous perimeter. She then reconsiders her consideration. To lie in wait to observe or capture "eventfulness" must surely border on the *em*pathetic.

Or is it better conceived as affective attunement? Her professorial concerns tend to infect her habitual activities.

She's sensitive to trends despite a senior status that often prejudices any hipness factor she secretly feels she deserves.

She's lately observed the becoming-fashionable of the term "empathy" in tandem with the now culturally inculcated understanding of "affect." There is something doing here though she can't put a finger on the impetus yet.

✳

Approaching the mirror in her bathroom as she has a hundred times in the past few days, she checks her cheek. The scabby strokes are each perceptibly turning a distinctive hue from left to right: violet-bluish, green, yellow-orangish, red. To her eyes it looks like the prismatic specter of a haunted event-to-come; a rainbow effect that elicits contagious potential.

Gazing with wide eyes at the reflected varicolor rat scratch, she again attempts to profile the perpetrator:

1. a rodent of the *Rattus rattus* variety
2. the common urban *Rattus norvegicus*

3. a disoriented pet guinea pig *Cavia porcellus*
4. a gerbil *Merionus unguiculatus*

One of these inflicted the scratch. Does the equation change if the perp was feral or domesticated? She was surely a perp herself — Caucasian, female, 176 cm, 50+, 63 kg — who with an astute defensive gesture, killed and/ or rendered comatose a member of the Rodentia order. Her culpability has become a tedious distraction, fuelling her hallucinations with disturbing after effects. Uneasy, uncertain, she reckons she must return to the scene of the crime. So awhirl is her worlding that she can't yet tell if this desire to return is a closure or a beginning.

Staring down the tubular structure of the POMOC she wonders what it is she hoped to find here? A teenage boy in orange tiger-striped tights skids past with such force she's sure he's enhanced his footwear with the alloy soles they sell online from the *Corridor* blog. Other skidders avoid her with precision or threaten certain collision with their inept technique. Her timing is off. The POMOC is so congested it reminds her of negotiating traffic in Cairo at midday, all nerve and insistence. Focusing on her own precarious balance, she misses the tactile grounding of the old-style travelators that once accommodated air-port passengers down endless gateways. She has yet to finesse the physics of the POMOC. She'll have to return at a quieter moment.

Her second attempt at epiphany yields different results. On a relatively quiet Saturday morning with few tasks waiting, she laced up a pair of red hi-top sneakers for better traction. Riding the force of compulsive instinct, she was out the door quickly. This time, she hoped to find a sparsely peopled corridor in which her thoughts could flirt with the milieu unimpeded. What then occurred in the center of this speed tunnel disturbed her already unstable equilibrium beyond rescue.

Once again inside, she attuned to the space, examining its every detail with acumen. She scratched at everything that shined, smelled the cleaning fluids that pervaded every corner. She hadn't noticed these things before. In sync with something uncanny, she listened to the plumbing, the ventilation unit, the air-con fans, heard the titanium whisper as it held its own against the gravity that tried to push its curves to earth. She listened to a distinctive peeping, pathetic yet robust, resonating in the dark whoosh of that half-kilometer long expanse. Near the fire extinguisher marker she could hear a high frequency modulation, fluctuating between a whimper and a zing. As she adjusted to its resonance, it filled the space of her skull with a pleasure she could not identify. A song of sorts, reverberantly emanated inside and outside her head and through the tensed limbs of her body. Entranced, suffused by the force of these sonic waveforms bouncing off her molecular being as so many interference patterns diffracted by particulate matter, she stood still to better feel what she heard – a riot of bifurcating forms, a cacophony of ambient noise threaded by a riveting virtuosic microtonal solo. Was the ghost of her victim haunting this place? Or does the rodent live to sing its aria, its own version of *Nessun Dorma* as an ironic joke that will agitate her already incessant sleeplessness? Can she alone hear what she thinks she hears?

Surely in her destabilized state she's reading an improbably vindictive narrative into the beautiful trilling.

Momentarily paralyzed in this incongruous space, she feels like Schrödinger caught in a sick illusion of profound dimensions. She came, as it were, to open the box, to bear witness to the dead or alive status of the rodent she affectionately thinks of as B⊗B. Can it be true that he is in superposition, living and not-living? The body, or trace of the body, is nowhere to be found of course. The incident occurred several days ago yet a voice persists. Fond of detective literature, she wonders if she's stepped into a world of virtual evidence, entered a mystery? A morality play, a slapstick comedy, a romantic telenovela? B⊗B must surely be or have been or will have been. Abruptly, she stops herself from constructing an unseemly anthropomorphic narrative. She's already overstepped her bounds by naming him. Taming him some would say.

Soon the ultrasonic frequencies fade into the hum of the background noise that swaddles every earthly environment – urban, pastoral. It's said there is no sound in space but Bette B doubts this. Sure, soundwaves as we know them require a molecular atmosphere to roll out their sonority. All the movement of gluey dark matter and the accelerating force of dark energy must relay some kind of a vibrational buzz our transductive hearing mechanisms cannot process. She imagines the operatic dissonance of an event horizon as it spirals the mouth of the black hole it will eventually nourish. Neither a Pythagorean nor a Nada Brahma disciple, she nonetheless imagines sound as ubiquitous. This instinct was supported in part by legions of manga artists who depict aural vibrations in the absence of sound. Star, smile, mistake, wrinkles, depression are all drawn as graphic cochlear perturbations.

Bette B takes comfort in the ineffable. Always has. It's perhaps why her aging ears, reduced to a limited 30–10,000 kHz bandwidth, can hear this plaintive rodent, vocalizing in the 30,000+ kHz range. Improbably, B⊗B's melody-free noise assertion stays with her even as her attention shifts to negotiating her skid to the exit.

Once outside the building, she decides to take a walk through a nearby park before returning home. She finds the hidden paths preferable to the asphalt thoroughfares of joggers, skateboarders, bikers, rollerbladers, power-walkers, daydreamers, dating couples, cheating couples, teenage gangs, senior clubbers, show-dog contenders, cold drink and hot coffee vendors – the spill of humanity and others out for a few deep inhales of freshly oxygenated air. Here is the reciprocity of photosynthesis at work amidst an army of respiring carbon machines. Allowing herself the fleeting image of taking B⊗B out for a walk, she wonders how other animals and humans would treat them both? Aborting her long stride, she stops to recall the rodent's features. Dark, grimy, short-haired with sharp incisors and a triangular snout. Or was it a mottled brown and dirty white with blunt front teeth and a pinkish snubby snout? She would fail miserably as a witness to an accident or celebrity sighting

Opening her eyes, she rummages through an interior pouch of her backpack searching for a round compact mirror she keeps for makeup emergencies. The spectral scratches have taken on a neon quality. Placing her bag on the remains of yellow snow nestled by the trunk of a barren elm tree, she reenacts her reflex gesture that afternoon. Passers-by must think she's practicing tai chi. She imagines the cold snout against her cheek, the scruffy whiskers, and now, filled with doubt as she is, feels tiny claws scrape her jaw in an effort to cling to her, to hold on to a pliable organic something in a blur of forbidding metals and plastics.

A Laryngeal Chronology

Franz Kafka, writer of short stories, letters, and novels died of starvation on 3 June 1924 from laryngeal tuberculosis. Eating had become too painful an exercise. One of his last works was the short story "Josephine the Singer and the Mouse Folk."

Giacomo Puccini, a chronic smoker, died on 29 November 1924 from throat cancer. He left the writing of his opera *Turandot*, featuring the famous tenor aria *Nessun Dorma* ("None may sleep"), unfinished.

On a winter morning in 1925, a singing mouse was discovered in Detroit, MI by JL Clark. This discovery would lead to significant biological research on the vocal physiognomy of rats. Recent scientific evidence supports the claim that some species of rodent do indeed produce song-like ultrasonic voicings similar to that of birdsong.

5

Interview with ShazDada, Part One

Transcribed and edited interview by Arts and Politics journalist ShazDada with Bette B on the POMOC *incident of 3 January. First published on the blog –* Situations.

SD: Thank you for agreeing to speak with me today regarding the now notorious incident in the POMOC. I know the readers of my blog will be fascinated to hear a depiction of the event from the horse's mouth so to speak.

BB: Happy to clarify things Shaz.

SD: Jumping right in then, could you first give us a bit of personal background ... your profile, your profession, etc.? I know you teach.

BB: Yes, well, I'm a female of a certain age, do I need to be specific?

SD: Not if you're uncomfortable sharing this information but I believe the popular press have already published the fact that you're 61, born in Illinois, single with no children, and a resident of City for over 30 years.

BB: [pause] Uhm, yes, that's correct. Thanks for clarifying for me.

SD: And what's your background, what do you do exactly?

BB: In my youth I was a singer in a rock 'n' roll band. Yeah, corny no? I later went into digital arts. For the past ten years or so I've been functioning as a quasi-academic, what they call an adjunct professor. Absolutely precarious labor I might add, in the field of, aah, well, we call it research creation.

SD: Huh?

BB: Yeah, it's also called artistic research. It's a stubbornly indefinable emerging niche for transversal artists primarily, who engage with discursive activity. That is to say feminist, gender, queer, post/decolonial, race theory, continental philosophy, you know. Not to forget the sciences … Aaah … that's not a very good explanation but it will have to do as a sound bite because it exhausts me to try and adequately explain it.

SD: Ok, yes, that's fine. Thank you. Moving on to the issue at hand. On 3 January you were in the renowned Corridor on the fourth floor of the infamously bizarre PostOffice building. What brought you to that location?

BB: That's a question I've asked myself many times. I'm an avid urban walker and I was out on a celebratory this-is-a-new-year-and-things-have-got-to-improve jaunt. You know, starting it off with a dérive-like exploration of City. You're sympathetic to that, the dérive I mean, I know from your blog entries.

SD: Indeed.

BB: There were few people on the streets that morning as many had the day off. The manic holiday energy had subsided to a kind of quiet sobriety on the streets. I like that. I don't know why I entered the PostOffice but it has an allure for sure. I thought to wander the mall area in the rotunda but I ended up on a shiny escalator in the rear of the south wing and kept ascending. I'd been to the POMOC once before – the Corridor – tried a few baby step skids. This seemed like a good moment to try again as it was unusually still and peaceful. Empty really.

SD: How did it go this time?

BB: Yeah, I stood at the end of the ... I guess it's the north end of the hallway for about five minutes before tentatively deciding to push off. Normally I wear decent walking shoes when out on a wander but that day I was wearing a pair of fabulous metallic leather flats and it all felt right somehow. I knew I was in the perfect shoes for the occasion.

SD: Did you know how to push off?

BB: Well, like many people, I'd read personal accounts of experiences in this place ... and there's that blog *The Corridor* that even has an instruction manual posted and then there's all those the *YouTube* videos ... so yeah, I knew to first assess the hallway for anchor points, look for the red fire extinguisher, the water fountain, and of course the midway handrail that everyone says are good stopping points. Landing sites. Then you pre-accelerate, bop, start from the right foot, push, then slide. That's what I did.

SD: And how was it?

BB: Well, you know ... thrilling, exhilarating, scary.

SD: When and where did you come to a stop.

BB: I'd decided to pull over at the midway handrail. It seemed the safest bet for a beginner.

SD: How did that go?

BB: Pretty well. I managed to stop what felt like an interstellar rocket ride but I fell on my ass trying to pin the landing. I'm in reasonably good condition for my age. I work out at the gym. Dance in my kitchen. I bounced back.

SD: Can you tell us what happened next?

BB: Yes, certainly. I went for another spin. The second time or maybe it was the third, I really flew. No ass bumps. I had to catch my breath I remember. Then I turned around to head back to the escalator when I perceived a movement. Something smallish was rocking back and forth and then whoosh it was coming toward me at great speed. I could soon make out that it was a rodent. A rat I thought, like the type you see everyday in the subways around here. It was having a lot of trouble with its balance, flopping around. At first I had to laugh. But then I realized it was headed directly at me. I panicked. Stood stock-still. Before I could catch another breath this creature was running up my leg, up my coat, up to my, my shoulder ... [pause]

SD: Whoa...

BB: Yeah. It "landed" on my left shoulder. I think it was as shocked as I was. And then I had a reflex reaction as far as I can remember. I felt its whiskers tickling my cheek and I grabbed it with a movement so quick I could never think myself capable of ... instinctively grabbed it ... by its neck, forcing its snout closed so it couldn't bite me. If I think about it now it must have been heavy, maybe close to a kilo, I don't know, three kilos, you know like maybe nine potatoes, but anyway, I squeezed its throat. I think I wanted to kill it. A survival reaction. Then something strange happened and I saw its color and shape morph from a dirty street rat to an adorable guinea pig, you know, the long hair type that are kind of cute and cuddly? It transformed as I was pushing on its windpipe. I just thrust its limp body away from me. It fell in the middle of the Corridor. I could see it was still shallowly breathing. I was in a state of shock, you know, utterly confused and shaky. I think I screamed for help. Yes, surely I did but it may have been one of those muted screams like the kind you have in dreams, you know, when you can't get the sound out. I think they call it sleep paralysis. You wake yourself gagging on a silent "Helllpp!"

SD: Was there anyone around? You said it was quite empty that day.

BB: Well that's just it. There was very little activity. I think there were some people at the far south end laughing and preparing to take a skid though that too might be a hallucination. As I said, I'm not sure I emitted noise of any kind. But oh yeah, there was this older couple. They were wearing oversized matching blue overcoats. They had a luggage cart with loads of storage boxes on it. I have no idea where they came from. They must have been behind me. I doubt they pushed off though. They were walking very carefully, slowly, in ice boots with heavy treaded rubber soles. They must have known this was perilous terrain. They asked if I was OK. Stared at the stunned rodent with me. I don't know what they saw. I think they whispered something to each other, said something to me, but I can't remember what it was. They left, slowly, I don't know, but anyway, they were strange, but they left. The animal was having a bit of twitchy muscle movement and I was suddenly afraid again. Then ... I left, like a hit-and-run driver. Only later did I become more terrified by my deed, my reaction, my cowardice, which seems in retrospect so violent and cruel ... I can't explain it. I've never been in a physical fight before. I don't really know how adrenaline works that way. But I was pumped full of it from my joyride that's for sure. Pumped up and apparently aggressively self-defensive. This confuses me a great deal and I haven't sorted it all out yet, haven't worked my way through the hormonal and ethical aspects. I'm still a bit stunned by the physical effects. But that's another story ...

SD: You returned home?

BB: Yeah, I poured myself a large glass of wine and collapsed on the sofa, or my reading chair, I'm not sure. After I was properly relaxed I went to have a look at myself in the bathroom mirror. I knew Mr. Rat had scratched my cheek and I knew I'd need a tetanus shot or worse. When I saw the marks I panicked yet again, this time with a visceral foreboding. I puked. It was yellowish.

SD: What did they tell you at the hospital?

BB: They told me I was brave. Ha! Then they gave me a tetanus shot and said it ought to do the trick but of course it would be best if I could bring the animal in for a check in case it was rabid. There's a series of injections for that and they thought it would probably be necessary. Inoculation or vaccination would be logical preemptive treatments but in my case if a virus was discovered then ... Of course me finding that specific rat now was out of the question. When I returned to the hospital several days later with my prismatic scarring they said that was an altogether unusual wound and that I might need a variety of antibacterial and/or antiviral drugs but they couldn't yet be sure. They take a few tubes of blood every week now along with tissue samples and stool samples. They're still working through a myriad of tests. Yesterday, they took DNA samples again, I have no idea why.

SD: When did the marks change to the neon glow they now have? Your left cheek is quite impressively singular I must say. At first glance one guesses you're inked with a hip new type of tat.

BB: Yeah, I'm aware. [pause] I call it "Tattarrattat" after James Joyce's famous palindrome for a knock on the door. You know, in *Ulysses*?

SD: Uh, no I didn't know that.

BB: Well, it's my way of making light of the situation, taking the ominous down a notch. *Tattarrattat.* Knock knock. A wake up call. [laughs]

SD: And the rodent body was never recovered?

BB: Apparently it regained consciousness and crept away.

SD: Are guys in hazmat suits looking for it? [chuckles]

BB: I believe that's an impossible task.

SD: OK. And what's the current status of the investigation?

BB: I'm under medical surveillance right now. They threatened quarantine but as no other symptoms have arisen, I'm still free to go about my life. I have to wear these latex gloves, carry around a bottle of Purello, and refrain from any intimate exchange of fluids.

SD: The gloves, they're red, and kind of kinky. [laughs]

BB: I'm aware. [giggles] I got them as a gift from a dominatrix friend of mine but didn't find a use for them until now.

SD: So the authorities are afraid you may have contracted a virus of some sort?

BB: They tested for the opportunistic pathogens. Bartonella, yeah, bubonic plague of course, something called hantavirus. Apparently they're still researching the possibility that it's a new strain of the Marburg virus but the results are inconclusive and I have none of the known symptoms such as a viral hemorrhagic fever ... thank God, that's a nasty bloody business. I brought some images I got from the lab with me if you want to put them on the blog. One microbiologist assigned to my case mentioned something about conducting an antibody micro-array analysis. There's an epidemiologist on the team as well. She's actually quite interesting, a scientist and a published novelist. We had a fantastic discussion about post-human aesthetics and radical empiricism. And ...

SD: Well, hmmm, I hate to cut you off but perhaps this is a good place to conclude our conversation for today. I don't want to exploit the time we agreed upon. I do want to thank you for this frank and insightful look into the POMOC event and naturally, I wish you a healthy recovery. Do you realize the color lines on your cheek glow with greater intensity when you're excited? They behave like a mood ring [giggles]. Anyway, I would love to invite you back for a second podcast interview session.

BB: Sure, there is much more to be told but in all honestly, I haven't yet digested what's happening to me. I don't know how to convey these things without seeming schitzy. I would love to come back another time to discuss this in more detail. When I'm ready ... you know, to speak about the more personal consequences and also share my thoughts on the many political ramifications of all this. I've been thinking a lot, reading ethical and new materialist theories, process philosophy, Whitehead's my favorite …

SD: Great. We'll set up another meeting then. Have a safe trip home and thank you Bette B.

BB: Thank you for inviting me Shaz.

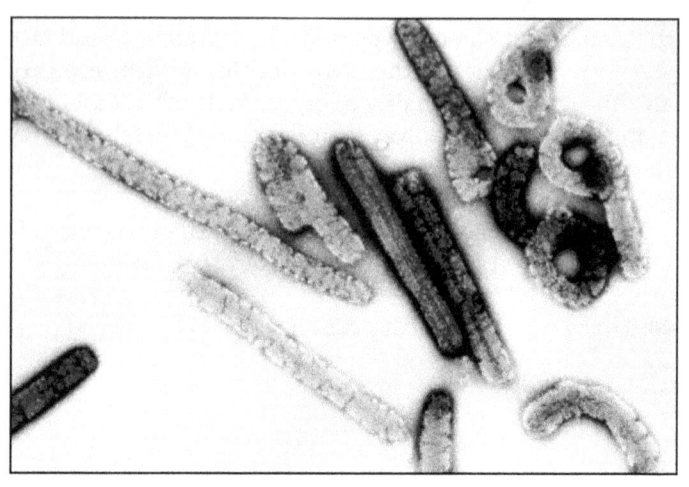

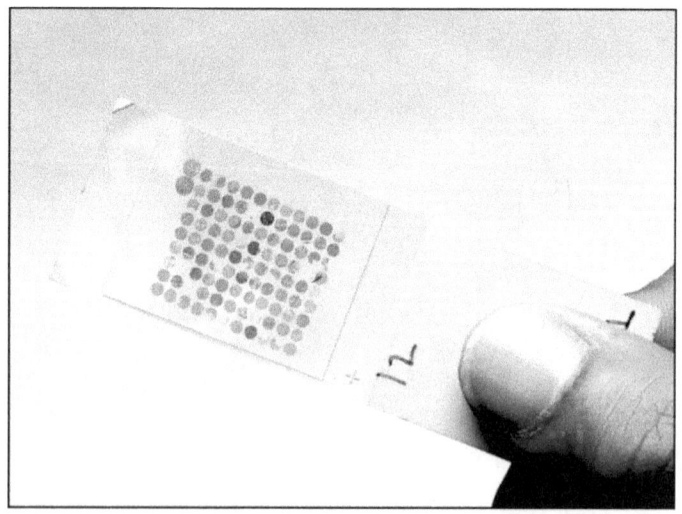

6

Hello Purello

It's the Purello that takes the most getting used to. There's a skewed reciprocity in the compulsive gesture of freshening one's hands in this way. The attempt to remove any bacterial trace from giving and receiving is futile. She supposes that in her circumstances this precaution is more than warranted, yet it feels slimy somehow, even as the stuff itself evaporates when it hits the air. The bottle wrapper says that it contains 63% ethyl alcohol, isopropyl alcohol, aminomethyl propanol, propylene glycol, and a myriad of other chemicals. She has no idea what these substances are but they "sound" toxic. Apparently regular old impure tap water is almost as effective in killing germs from human hands, but since her condition is precarious she's become obsessively antiseptic compulsive. Surprisingly, the latex gloves add a fashion wallop to her wardrobe and she loses little dexterity due to their flexibility. The main annoyance is the smartphone handicap. She's considered punching a tiny hole in each thumb. It would alleviate that inconvenience but then she will have rendered the gloves partially ineffective. She hasn't decided yet how to handle this situation. Already stretched to the limits of her coping ability, Bette B is now preoccupied with identifying islands of stability rather than attending to the many instabilities in her heightening perception of a whirling, indeterminate world.

She recalls a factoid. As a species we're most human at the moment of birth when our cellular material is purely *Homo sapiens*. By the time we're mature adults we have accrued so many diverse bacterial cells that, if one were to make a corporeal analogy, only the area from the foot to the knee of one leg would be composed of distinctly human cellular matter. The rest is other.

This analogy has long impressed her. It puts an effusive spin on categorical animality. She'd chuck the gloves and the Purello if she were alone in this. Get on with the getting on. The threat of her contaminating agency keeps sociability in check. As for the intimate exchange of bodily fluids, her aging, drowsy libido offers little resistance to restrictions. She has more time on her red hands.

So naturally, Bette B's become inordinately interested in all things pathogenic. She's fastidiously searched through digital and analog archives on the history of infectious disease control. Confused by distinctions between inoculation and vaccination, she looked into the etymologies of the terms.

Inoculate (v):

mid-15c., "implant a bud into a plant," from Latin inoculates [...] "graft in, implant," from *in-* "in" + *oculus* "bud," originally "eye." Meaning "implant germs of a disease to produce immunity" first recorded (in inoculation) 1714, originally in reference to smallpox. After 1799, often used in sense of "to vaccine inoculate" [*OED*].

To graft a bud, an eye. It reminded her of teratoma tumors, a subject she was afraid to research.

She was surprised to find that a "vaccine," initially, was cowpox. *Vacca* = cow. The Latin root was a giveaway but she hadn't been paying attention.

Vaccination (n):

1803, used by British physician Edward Jenner (1749-1823) for the technique he devised of preventing smallpox by injecting people with the cowpox virus (*variolae vaccinae*), from vaccine "pertaining to cows, from cows" (1798), from Latin *vaccinus* "from cows," from *vacca* "cow" [*OED*].

Whereas differentiating between the bacterial and the viral is a vital clarification, inoculation, vaccination, and immunization are used interchangeably among the folk who actually do these things. She wonders what the team of researchers handling her case might call her antidote should they need to contrive a preemptive fix? Rattusination? Gerbillination? How would they extract the cellular material without the culprit? A little ashamed of her ignorance in these matters, she's determined to be a quick study in all things microbial.

One takeaway insight resonated with her usual interests. The zoomorphic. Why had she never noticed the exaggerated use of animal references in human language before? Descriptive adages, similes, categorizations so endemic to the quotidian that they pass as unremarkable, appearing regularly as people, as institutions, as markets, as corporations, as products, as insults; weaving their way through conversations in all tongues as a subliminal nature/culture membrane. Now an ultra-sensitive witness to the zoological, she fancies herself shaman material, feels a lightning rod of recognition as she squirts another round of ridiculous purifier on her hairy hands.

Zoomorphic

An avid hyperlinker, Bette B spends admittedly too much time locked in the throes of search engines. One peripheral thread worth following however concerns zoomorphic research. Noting the plethora of animal metaphors and similes and their often pejorative use as a framing of "the other" she clicked around the web for insight. One study cataloged generalizations of over thirty animal types referenced in common dictionaries. She culled a few from Somner and Somner:

Dog: Someone disliked or ugly. An offensive prison guard; an inferior player. Can also be used playfully as a term of affection.

Horse: A diligent, able student. A term of high regard and esteem. A strict disciplinarian. A stupid, rude, stubborn, contemptible person. A corrupt prison guard.

Mouse: An informer. A girlfriend, sweetheart or wife. A harlot.

Rat: A despised person. An informer.

7

Knock Knock

According to a prominent search engine, a high-ranking site for Knock Knock joke aficionados lists these as among the funniest in their top ten:

4. Knock knock.
Who's there?
Interrupting cow.
Interrup-MOOOOOOOO!

8. Knock knock.
Who's there?
Cows go.
Cows go who?
No, cows go moo!

10. Knock knock.
Who's there?
Interrupting doctor.
Interrup-You have cancer.

Bette B feels these entries are unfunny. To be honest, she doesn't get numbers 4 and 10 at all. And why the focus on cows? This she finds mysterious, adding fuel to her developing interest in animal metaphors and vaccines.

She decides to invent her own infinitely regressive loopy version of what was most likely never a humorous joke format. A fan of the doggedly ambiguous, her contribution to the form is similarly unfunny but nonetheless leaves her mildly amused.

Tattarrattat.

Tattarrattat.

Tattarrattat.

Tattarrattat.

(*ad infinitum*)

8

Who's There?

Holed up, nursing his wounds, B⊗B's been revisiting what he thinks of as his epiphanic moment, his near death experience on the Path. In countless ways, its impact upon him continues to reverberate. He's exhaustively retraced his steps and stumbles that day in an attempt to piece details together; in a frustrated effort to come to some kind of understanding of his character, motivations, desires, and on some metaphysical plane, his beliefs. His cousin has accused him of pursuing answers through transcendental means. Gettin' religious and all. But this is her whacked out, semi-anaesthetized sensibility talking. Her radar is way rusted. Ethanol can do that. Nonetheless, his endless rehashing has begun to simulate a style of storytelling a victim engages in with the authority of a parent, a journalist or perhaps a god. One version goes something like this:

It was late, or early, depending on one's perspective. I was taking a risk by being out in the open after dawn, in all the brightness of the morning. I'd been licking aggressively that evening, consuming more of the happy vapor than usual. Why? That's a question I can't answer honestly because it's complicated. Or complex. I'm not sure which term best contextualizes my state on that day. Actually I have no idea why I was where I was. I had been out playing late, or early, and continued to play. Sometimes one does things inexplicably, without purpose, without intention. I don't tend to psychologize my every motivation. I leave that activity to other species.

I've been trying to master the skid recently. Well, master is too ambitious a word for my futile attempts at maintaining an upright posture while gliding several centimeters above the ground surface. It also has unfortunate overtones so maybe "wizard a skid" works better? Hazard a skid? Anyway, humans and larger animals can better direct their balance at these unnatural speeds. The first time I tried I could feel my hands and back feet leave the surface of the Path altogether. I thought I would be flung against the far wall of the long hall but somehow the momentum decreased proportionate to the space, I magically decelerated as the boundary approached, coming to a soft stop. I was quite a distance from the Hole in the storage room that shuttles my entry to and from this world.

Still amateur at this, I practice when the space is unpeopled. On this occasion it was empty but for a solitary human draped in black like a shadow with the most fantastic shiny, reflective footwear I have ever seen. I couldn't take my gaze off them. The light bouncing erratically from the curvilinear polished surfaces of the interior walls blindingly diffracted around the touch of those shimmering feet upon the glistening ground. It was terrifyingly attractive this light, so bright as to blind one like me, pull my kind by the sheer force of their brilliance. Without further consideration, I was off in skid mode, my momentum increasing. Distracted by the bright-bright, I felt panic swell as I lost my balance all together, flopping from side to belly at a ridiculous speed. The lure of those shoes threw my equilibrium out of sync.

The glittery foot figure had stopped still near the rail that runs along the middle of the Path but there was no friction or object to slow my own way forward. I could zip by this human, but having no hope of gaining traction in my present state of uncontrolled corporeal thrust, the thick, vertical fabric of her outer clothing (for I could now smell her sex) promised a gripping respite from a splattered death against the far wall. I did what I must do, directed all my effort towards ascending that dark cylindrical rise of textured folds in a milieu of spectral light and glare. Whatever might occur, it could not but be magnificent, wrapped as it was in such an aura.

Up I went in a nanosecond, vaulted from the shoe welt to the glimmering contour of the cow-leather upper and up again to the reassuring feel of thick materiality, and finally to the peak of vulnerable flesh. I clung to a supple smoothness that I know now was the soft, finely wrinkled skin of her cheek. My heart stopped beating. There was no next move. It was her turn.

And she took it. As one might expect, she reacted with animal instinct. With a wild blitz of motion she would rid herself of the present danger, of the parasite clinging absurdly to her upper body. As she held my jaws between her sheepwooly hands and began to squeeze all breath from me, I could feel the direct pressure on my voice box, the crushing of the vibrating lips that let the song out. Even in a conflating moment of life and death, a dark irony cast a balm over the pain. My eyes closed, I saw nothing of what I felt through every cell of my wriggling body as all sense of being there vanished.

I have no recollection of hitting the floor. No clue as to the length and breadth of my unconscious state. I recall attending to the slowly receding flicker I now suspect was the luminous footwear that first attracted me. I took a strange comfort in that recognition; in the fading echo of the click, click, click of heel to floor. More unsettling was the blurry sighting of the boxy blue forms that silently crept towards the vanishing point of my perspective. Blue devils. Their presence, though waning, excited a blitz of fear sufficient to force my aching body upright. I began a slow, painful crawl from the center of the Path to the relative safety of the plinth along the wall. From here, with luck, I could make my way unnoticed to the refuge of the Hole.

This story could and will be told several times in many ways, unfolding with a curious Rashomon *effect. The thoughtful reconstituting of B⊗B's own experience exhibits a surprising dexterity of worldview. He continues as though speaking to another audience:*

I have no means of comparing my Rodentia sense of timespace to that of other species. In my way, I am careful not to project the perception and affection of my realities onto the felt sensations of other's realities. Such projections are tinged with arrogance and always get me in trouble. I am aware that I don't know what I don't know as keenly as I do know what I don't know. I tend to accept difference in itself and leave it at that as I move on to the next morsel, the next high, the next voicing, the next skid. It seems like a chronological sequence or maybe a choreographic score – a birth-to-death series of tiny events, some charged, some flat, most necessary, some blissfully unnecessary yet ever so satisfying. Especially since that encounter, I have wondered about the differing range and qualities of affective attunement between species, between things, between cousins, between, say, a grape seed and a bottle cap, a steel screw and a puddle of hot piss, a tendency and a constraint?

How can I grasp what she felt that day without falling prey to a species-specific worldview? Now I realize humans do this all the time, anthropomorphize, they can't help themselves even though they're supposedly smart enough to know better. The jury is out on this problem – hung. I can gauge the intensity of trans-species survival instincts; of a choke and a swat and the urgency of flight much better than I can the irrational lure of the bright-bright diffraction of those damn shoes that threw me off my game that morning. Living, it would seem, entails the orderly distillation of sensation, indeterminately cast into the chaosmos that provides its very oxygen.

All that said, I am left with the uneasy yet exhilarating feeling that we two have somehow mingled; now share common agents that do their immanently microcosmic work in our very different architectures of being. What passed between us that day may well be more than matter. It may be something that comes to matter. And yes, I know that's a lightweight pun but I utter it because I feel it occurring. Why? How? I just somehow knew she'd return to the scene. And she did.

Some time, not much, passed. I was weak but I summoned enough energy to hobble back through the Hole to a shadowy corner near the Path exit. Before indulging in a necessary period of hermetic restoration, I needed to sniff out the traces of what had occurred. Give myself something to think about during my lonely recovery. As I hid in the shadows of the Path I knew she too was near. I sensed she too was wary, sniffing. Instinctively, without agitation, I opened my mouth, my conviction amplified perhaps by my drugged state of Spiritus pain sublimation. As I puffed up my chest cavity with deep inhales, my tortured vocal folds emitted what I can only describe as dissonant sonorities that frankly, shocked me. *Gyo.* The tonal qualities, in concert with the sheer exertion of expression, were like nothing I have ever heard or produced. I can't quite believe they vibrated solely from my body, from the sorely injured tissue substrates of my folds. The point I'm getting at is – she heard me. This is a biological impossibility of course, human hearing cannot ordinarily exceed 20 kHz and that's a pleasure only young humans imbibe in. Reactively agile though she is, she is most definitely no longer young. Besides, the extraordinary bandwidth of my voice that day, cracking and fluctuating though it was, spun out to heights that challenged the limits my own ability to feel sound. Something is doing. Something peculiar is afoot.

Now curled into a ball of filthy fur, squeezed into a secure pocket of his burrow, B⊗B recuperates. This will take some time. Free to brain wander, his rat thoughts turn from the solitary figure of the statuesque woman to the forbidding menace of the blue ones.

9

The Blue Ones

What was it about these blue ones that so terrified him? They had stoic, feature free faces as far as B⊘B could read "featureless" through a maze of spotted, deeply creviced epidermal membrane. He'd inhabited the PO complex often enough at off-peak hours to understand something of their frequent comings and goings. Having the look of weary travelers or civil servants, a cuckoo couple on a stroll, they exacted total indifference in passers-by, human and other-than. Their imperceptibility drew his keen curiosity, as they exuded a state of being hovering somewhere between a not-yet displaced and soon-to-be disappeared. The bland transparency of their presence, even as they struggled with the industrial grade moving cart on their slow walks through the building, could not disguise the weight of inevitability that hung from their heavy coats whose large interior pockets, he knew, held their daily stash of edibles.

B⊘B had witnessed them often in the rotunda picking through the same disposables that whet his own appetite: spongy Twinkie bits, stale French fries, peanut butter slabs, sugary doughnut holes, yellow bits of scrambled eggs and leathery chicken wing remains. In a sense, they were competitors for the spoiled spoils of the accelerated ones.

He'd been spying on others like them, this particular breed of the dispossessed. Wrapped in relics of military issue outerwear from powdery blue to the deepest ultramarine, they inhabited City's non-places much as he himself did. Necessary scavengers, bottom feeders. They were the un-bred, conceived through chromosomal happenstance. The Blue Ones were the most conspicuous contrast to designer GenTels, an advertising euphemism of the most obnoxious sort. (GenTel being the popular acronym for the Genetic Teleology Corps, the eugenics conglomerate that merged their research laboratories with Pharmakos Pharmaceuticals towards the end of the last century.) With the exploding global mandate for designer progeny, GenTel's engineering research centers required an enormous surfeit of test subjects. These specimens, of which *Rattus norvegicus* was in particularly high demand, were supplied almost entirely by an international cadre of blue ones.

Privately, they referred to themselves as Tuaregs. Unaware of inappropriate appropriation it brought them heightened self-esteem, adorned their abject situation with a solid nomadic attitude they could take pride in. They were conspicuous because of the equipment they laboriously lugged around to accomplish the task that would put food in their bodies three, sometimes four times a week. B⊗B knew, as did the whole of his tribe, their profession. They were the Rat Catchers.

B⊗B was certain these two had been present at his epiphany. He knew they carried nets, cages, ultrasonic emitters, poisoned arrows, tasers, tranquilizer guns, pan pipes, and flutes of every material type (wooden, silver, steel, aluminum, alloy). The coup de grâce, their weapon of mass destruction, was a semi-sedated Bull Terrier pup trained in the blood sport of rat-baiting. They'd named him Billy in adoring reference to the prodigious nineteenth-century raticide champion, a cross-species legend who could dispose of over 100 rats in well under six minutes. Blue Billy was carted along for occasions when all other techniques were deemed inappropriate or likely to fail. B⊗B could tell the keepers had come become fond of this mutt.

In this particular pockmark of timespace the blue ones are required to wear a pink badge with the letters **PC** inscribed in Helvetica Bold font. B⊗B is aware this stands for Pest Control, the post-postmodern facelift of a profession as old as prostitution. The semiotic genealogy of this identifier functions as a ridiculous teaser. He's noticed that quite often, the blue ones bury the badge away in a pocket. He figures its invisibility offers them some semblance of being off-duty in an always-on world.

That must have been the case that day on the Path. They left him there, foregoing a tidy bit of compensation, badges deep inside their crumb-caked pockets. Did they know they had passed by a queer specimen, the celebrated Sounder, a perfect case study for a doctoral candidate in Applied Health Sciences or worse, a contestant for an illegal rat-baiting ring? Did they know, or think they knew, the character of that stunned rat body, leaving him to escape or expire on a coin toss of fate? Were they hyper-alert that morning or dull tired? Had they attuned to his species? Had they developed a wavering empathy?

Content to speculate, to create one viable scenario out of many possibilities, B⊗B chose, as is his want, in the affirmative. He granted them an animal sensibility of fair play he suspected was often dormant in humans. Generally speaking, in the nonhuman view a hunt is a hunt, a predator a predator, a kill a kill, a meal a meal. No tears, no wringing of paws, claws, or tendrils. Though there are exceptions of course, moral coding is unambiguous.

The human species has complicated the planet with the evolution of relativistic ethics. He has tried to wrap his head around human behavior patterns but can make little sense of their inconsistencies. B⊘B's type long ago adapted to the indeterminate inevitabilities of mortality.

10

Real Hallucination

Once back home she collapsed into the comfort of her reading chair. After hastily shopping for sustenance supplies, denuded of the racy latex gloves and camouflage headscarf, Bette B licked her hands. Having squeezed a plop of Purello on her palms and given them a brisk rub, she's taken to licking them clean, finger by slick finger. There's an unpleasant aftertaste but once accustomed to its bitter sting, the buzz offers a quite singular jolt. In fact, if pressed, she'd have to describe the sensation as similar to the initial ping one feels when pushing off in the Corridor; that heady, intoxicating synthesis of decisiveness and the out-of-control that accompanies a "what if."

What she would not say in this description, what she'd keep to herself out of embarrassment and a contrived sense of decency, is that she takes as much pleasure in licking her fingers clean as she does the alcoholic buzz it engenders. Perhaps it's the ironic paradox that accompanies the act that amuses her, eggs her on in an unspoken complicity. It's the delicious transfer of the 500 or so odd bacteria that coat every human tongue to her antiseptically protected hands, in a perverse cleansing gesture, that thrills her. How many species bathe this way she wonders? That she can't see the microscopic, swarming activity every lick perpetuates enhances the gesture's wild relevance. Like a Wiccan offering, it thrusts her into the tumult of belief and disbelief structures. She horse jumps, thinking thoughts at right angles to the expanding infinities of cosmologies and quanta, of ghosts and dust, of monsters and pets.

Absently, lost in starry haze of unseeable charm quarks, she gives a final über-hygienic lick to her right pinky finger. She's back to a tactile reality, reconsidering the double agency of the Purello, part purifier, part hallucinogen. A quasi substance if ever there was one. How is it, she wonders, that the all-too-anthropocentric, semi-psychotic, vari-phobic, disinfectant, cultural ritual of ridding nature from flesh has become an urban obsession, a medical necessity, an anti-contaminate sensibility? Sure, deadly plague-like infectious disease is passed to humans through animals. Rats > Bubonic, Chimps > HIV, Fruitbats > Ebola. These are the hypotheticals of biological science, built upon the historical dynamism of "facts," those slippery bits of data that hold a position of "truth" for a while and gradually succumb to entropic erosion like just about everything else humans think they know. She doesn't get the nature/culture rupture at all. Never did. Squirting another round of Purello on her hands, she licks its residue more aggressively now. She's seeing things, seeing things otherwise.

In a moment of oneiric clarity, Bette B recalls a recent event she'd scribbled into her lucid dreaming journal. The desire to examine the entry overtakes her. Standing up a bit too quickly, she steadies herself from a dizzying headspin. Breathing deeply, she grabs the notebook from the bed stand and flips to an entry from 5 November:

Dusty, matted with years of whatever it is that gets into the seams, creases, cracks, and texture of objects over time, this weathered SLR film camera of no particular brand was owned and used regularly by a professional photographer. It came load-ed with a roll of black and white 35 mm film; the type, age, and ASA were unknown to me. The camera was shoved into my hands by an older man with shoulder-length white hair and a grumpy disposition. He reminded me of a shaman, a Don Juan, or the di-rector of an art school. The gesture was meant as a provocation, a challenge and a threat; the task was to shoot exemplary ad-vertising images of various models of horse-driven chariots and wagons from a luxury vehicular company. Something unspoken was at stake, probably my career. On a dirt track outside the alu-minum structure that housed the studio equipment and dark-room of the deceased photographer, I opted to shoot the seven horse and carriage types as they ran at breakneck speed toward my position in the middle of the racing lane. The 180 mm tele-photo lens was stuck fast with the accumulated gunk of years in the threaded body casing. As the pounding flesh, metal, and creaking wood approached, I snapped the wild eyes and drool-ing mouths of horse and human as they rushed towards me. Having calculated their approximate distance and speed, I was able to leap from the path of the oncoming tonnage just in time, each time. Any hesitation or klutzy stumble could prove fatal. I repeated this feat seven times with varying actors, models, and athletes in the role of horse, rider, and wagoner. I hoped for decent photographic results but wasn't sure how to get the film from the camera body once I'd finished shooting as it was sealed closed by the residue of time.

This being the far riskier aspect of the assignment and terrified I'd expose or damage the celluloid images, I suspended the task and hopped a small water taxi. I arrived at a former warehouse that now served as a collective studio space for interdisciplinary artists including my old friend Babs whom I hadn't seen in dec-ades. She was working tech for the performance installation of some celebrity artist. The concrete floor of the workspace was lit-tered with lighting equipment, cables, projectors, theater props, and lunch leftovers from the past week. In this black-box set-ting, a bright white light lit up a five-meter section of the floor in what appeared to be the center of the space. Several people were gathered, sitting, squatting, or standing around on the cold concrete. I joined them, curious about the small black elliptical objects that sometimes sped through the brilliant light and over the laps and feet of the concentrating spectators. From a seated perspective I realized with a small jolt that the objects were rat bodies, scurrying over, under, and around the laser light beam. The other guests had adjusted to the initial shock of holographic rodents running over their limbs. As I relaxed and enjoyed the realistic and startling speed of these virtual creatures, a palpable sense of anxiety spilled through the installation as one of the rat figures seemed to be slowly morphing into a "real" rat as it scurried in and out of the light. Indeed, the figure now had weight, form, hair, whiskers, and smelled vaguely animal. Several seated and squatting humans screamed and jumped to stand. Some ran. Having just been rushed seven times by living, snorting horses I was less inclined to fear and kept a grip on the performative context of the event though the effect was decidedly angina inducing. Was this animal presence outside the control of the "work," a likely occurrence in this location? Was it a magical technological feat I knew Babs was capable of pulling off? I wasn't yet in enough of a contemplative state to value the aesthetic experience. I was overcome by a raw sensation of sensation itself.

Here Bette B's journal entry for 5 November ends. She has no desire to continue reading other entries. This is enough agitation for one day. She grabs the Purello again to clean whatever contaminate might have jumped to her hands from the journal. It's an excuse of course, for liberating her mind.

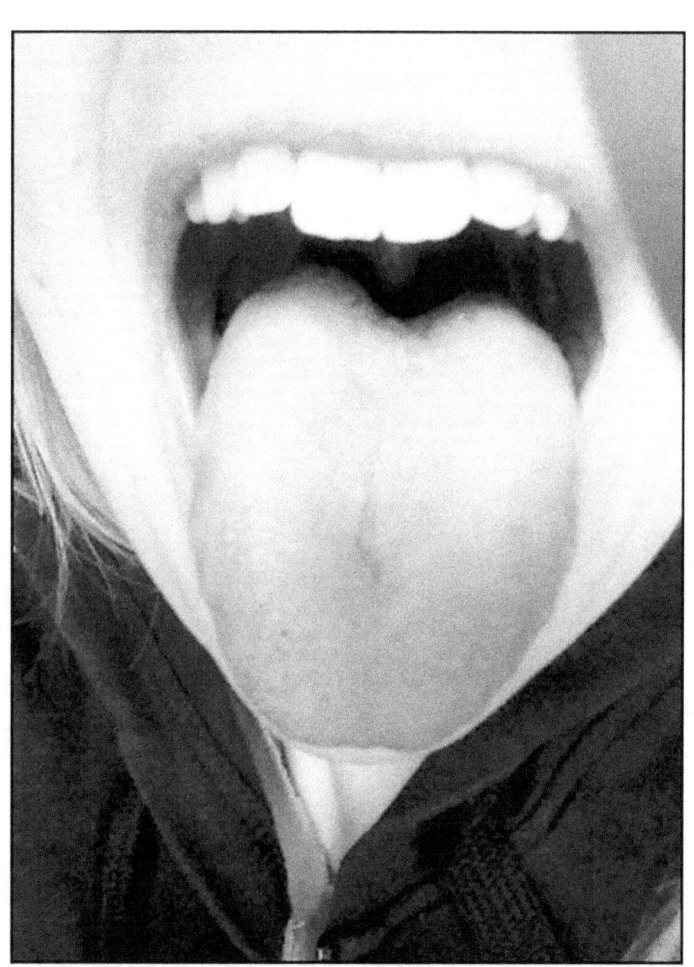

11

Quasimodo

All was in ordered disorder. *Tattarrattat,* or "RatTat," wasn't showing any signs of disappearing, maintaining a healthy glow. The latex continued to suffocate her hands. She was teaching herself to attack a keyboard with limited sensation in her fingertips, causing more typos than usual. But she was getting the hang of it.

On this fine afternoon of bursting spring green and yellow crocus, she searched for online diagnoses of spectral scarring symptoms, and basically anything she can find on rats. She's been at this for more than two months but today she happens on a provocative hyperlink. Transfixed, she copy–pastes some excerpts to her digital notebook:

CHAMPAIGN, Ill. — At the University of Illinois, a new study claims that in order to reduce a loss of vocal intensity in the muscles of the aging larynx, older rats train their vocal folds. This condition called presbyphonia is faced by many humans as they age. In a young, healthy larynx the vocal folds completely open and close during vibration. This creates little bursts of air we hear as sound. Aging causes degeneration in the muscle, resulting in a weakened voice that becomes easily fatigued by the efforts to communicate.

[...]

Vocalizations of the rat species are ultrasonic and therefore above the range of human hearing. Through the use of special recording techniques that lower their frequency, humans are able to perceive rat calls. These sounds are similar to birdsong. In studying human vocal characteristics, rats are ideal subjects as they vocalize with similar neuromuscular mechanisms.

Images of rat studies of all types are plentiful online. She's taken to printing them and pinning them up on the wall opposite her desk, an old habit from her studio years. They provide graphic evidence of the laboratory testing that buoys the superficially uplifting context of the "singing rat" project. All the ethical conundrums ping-ponging in her head come out to play. She stares at the flayed images of rat organs. Her sense of smell, lately hyper-accentuated to the point of extreme discomfort within a four meter range of any dumpster, pissoir, or perfumed woman, kicks into her imaginary as the scent of formaldehyde mingles with the Tibetan incense she burns to mask a profusion of scents she has not yet learned to tolerate.

Circumspect, she removes the gloves and squirts another drop of Purello on her hands for comfort. This action is by now obsessive compulsive but she can't worry about the pathological consequences as she closes her eyes and feels the billion cells of her body dying and dividing, feels the scavenger macrophage cells devouring the dead ones. She's exfoliating at an accelerated pace or so it seems when her tongue advances to her forearms, biceps, and shoulders in her extended ritual. She is, for now, a tribe of one, inculcated by masses of other ones, on the move. She is *quasi*. Almost. Quasimodo. She says it out loud. "Quasimodo!" It rings true.

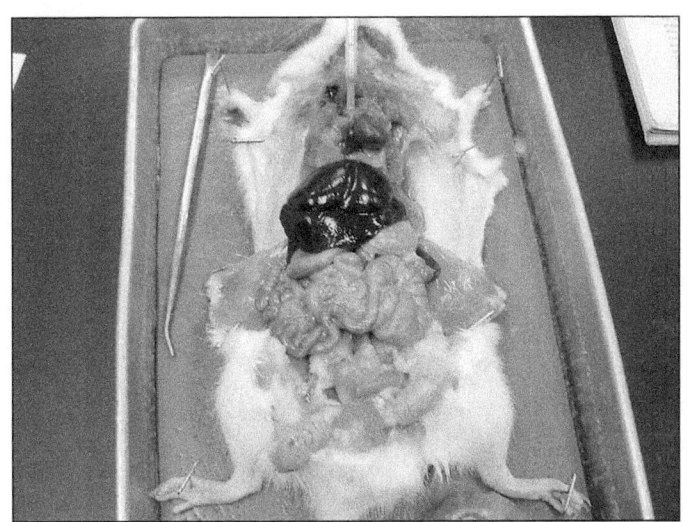

Quasi-modo

A quick search on the hunchback monster and finds his etymological origin in the Latin: *Quasi modo geniti infants,* literally "as if in the way newborn babes crave rational milk without treachery".

Cute. Absurd?

Quasimodo = as if in [this] manner

Or better:

Quasimodo = what if in [this] manner?

Or:

Quasi-modo: what if, almost but not yet, in this way.

12

The Dark Precursor

As the weeks pass, Bette B has resigned herself to manifest change at its most indisputable. She can cover the blotchy patches of thickening hair on her legs and arms with appropriate clothing. Or take a razor to it. Or visit a wax bar. Anxiety has become a permanent condition peppered with frequent scratch attacks on her own flesh and any material object in her vicinity. Her tactile curiosity intensifies in pace with her sensitivity to hearing and smell. Even the way she moves around her apartment is exaggerated now as she dashes to the toilet and darts to the door. The pronounced skittish tics in her head and shoulders are of the wary type, on perpetual look out.

RatTat operates like many fashionista ornaments: the piercings, jewelry, henna tattoos, and accoutrements of urban costume. Millennials are particularly lavish, at least to her face, with their kudos. As one put it, "the elegant calligraphic gesture of the spectral strokes in tandem with the brilliant dynamic flux of fluorescence is so dope". Though some peripheral friends evasively distance themselves, she feels more adored than abhorred. For now, she keeps to herself as much as possible and waits. Expectant.

The journal she's been keeping documents her encounters with the variegated realities of daily existence. It's

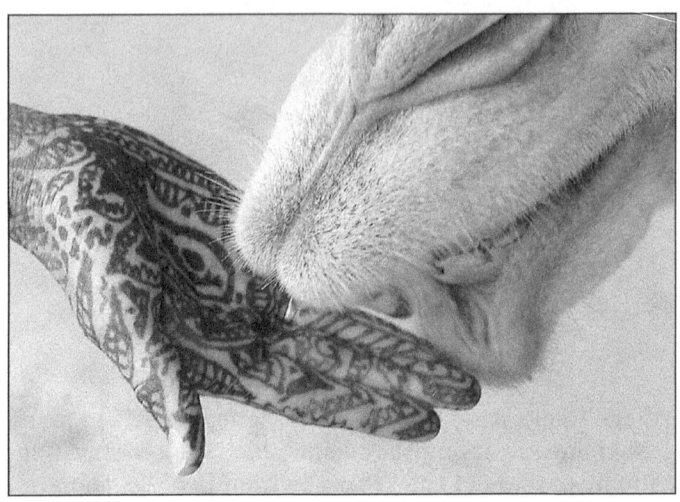

proved to be both a solace and a surprise. The 24-hour cocktail of waking life and somni-life explodes in the brainspill that rushes from immobilized REM atonia to hyperactive scribble every morning as she jolts to life. For 178 consecutive days she's recorded this in-between spacetime. Like well-kneaded dough, she folds futures and pasts, thinking and the unthought, into every entry. Absently flipping through the entries, she re-reads an anecdote from a conference excursion last September:

I'm on a train from Copenhagen to Aarhus, riding backwards from the ruins into the future like Walter Benjamin's Angelus Novus. "His eyes are wide, his mouth is open, his wings are spread." Sitting opposite me is a twenty-something Danish man in a black zip-up all-weather jacket, immersed in the glare of his laptop. Many people refuse to take a seat on the train facing the vantage of their departure, backs to the future. It disorients, gives a sensation of unease, or nausea. These folks insist on facing forward to meet what's forthcoming head on as it passes them by. Personally, I've never had an uncomfortable visceral experience while riding backwards and often prefer a good long look at what I'm leaving behind.

This brief passage strikes her given the intensity of "changling" perceptions these past few months. Other notably banal passages produce similar intrigue. Lurking between the lines of automatic writing lays her quest for a peek at the imperceptible movement of her favorite mystery being, the dark precursor. It's a topic she frequently alludes to though it's clear she hasn't formed a coherent idea of this thing. In the very first journal entry for instance, she reads from an extended reverie on the relevance of dream states. In her near illegible script, she writes that this figure of the dark precursor: *tends towards simultaneously generating ~~divergent histories~~ multiplicities relational events. The ~~becomings~~ impulsions of past child and future adult are overlaid ~~in superposition [potential]~~, in quantum effect ... here, there, everywhere, nowhere, before, after ... microperceptions swish and snag in the folding. As the dark precursor goes about its surreptitious business, shit happens and then you die. Events flash and pop as PAAF! and BOOM! and then ... emergence emerges as something different. What the fuck!*

Leafing through the scratchy traces of last year, she finds these offhand conjectures amusing and oddly reassuring though she doubts she fully grasps her own musings. What is this thing, or no-thing she calls potential anyway? She thinks it oscillates between stuff, between PAAFs and BOOMs, reds and blues, tires and gravel, desire and pain. If she tries to pin potential down to a definition it's no longer what it might become. Her brain hurts, her face is swollen, her feet cramp. Strewn with piles of paper clippings, cut-outs, magazines, moldy cheese chunks, and cracker dust, she dives beneath the duvet on her futon, spilling the guts of reconnaissance and sustenance around the room. Opening her eyes to absorb the diffused light passing through the paisley patterned linen of her bedware, she obliquely feels "potential" affects the nebulous activity that communicates difference between the different. Finding a piece of yesterday's croissant in her hair, she snacks, re-considering the curiosity that is the unseen force convolving dark matter and dark energy into a palpable magical, alchemical protagonist. Drum-roll, cymbal crash, voilà! Bring on the black-cape shebang of *The Dark Precursor!*

Still tracing the spermy, teardrop pattern on the bedcov-er, she recalls how she once caricatured this black-caped figure as a faux Marvel Comics superheroine with the nick *ZeNeZ*, a palindrome for quirky zigzagging qualities. The tipsy middle "N" snakes between a Zen dynamic and a French nose. She had attempted to create a conceptual comic strip but eventually abandoned the experiment. Under cover this morning, it's the nosey reference that tickles her immediate attention again.

What was meant as an epistemological irony has be-come a weird portent. Scrambling from her bed she ri-fles through a stack of plastic binders on a bookshelf and pulls out a laser print of the first and only issue of her zine – *ZeNeZ* and the *RE[a]DShift Boom!* Reading through the obscure thought bubbles, a factive mix of science and poetry, she recalls with a start, the philosopher's muted warning: "the dark precursor is not a friend."

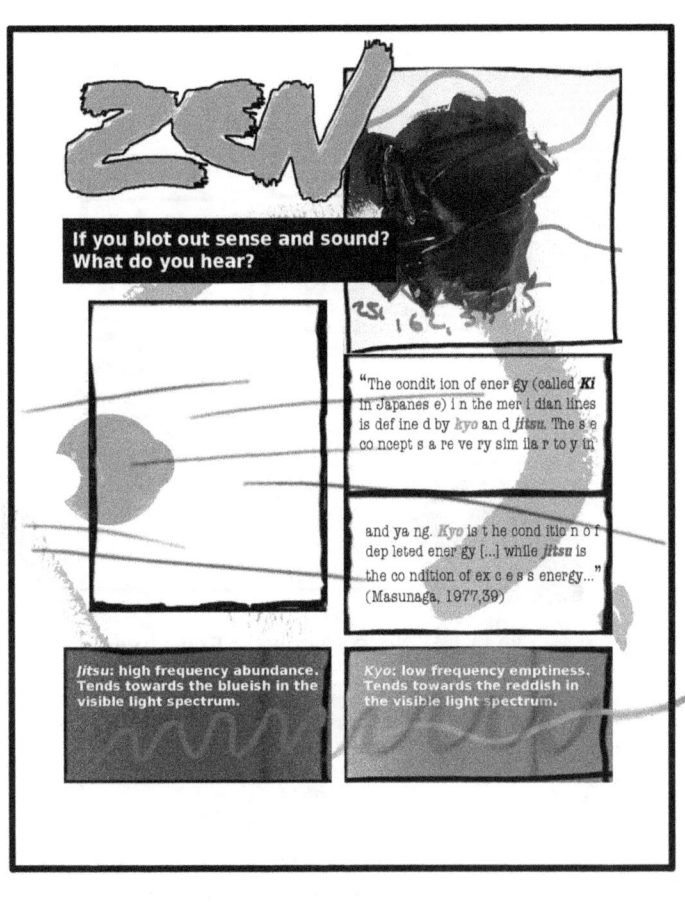

ZEN

**If you blot out sense and sound?
What do you hear?**

"The condit ion of ener gy (called *Ki* in Japanes e) i n the mer i dian lines is def ine d by *kyo* an d *jitsu*. The s e co ncept s a re ve ry sim ila r to y in

and ya ng. *Kyo* is t he cond itio n o f dep leted ener gy [...] while *jitsu* is the co ndition of ex c e s s energy..." (Masunaga, 1977,39)

Jitsu: high frequency abundance. Tends towards the blueish in the visible light spectrum.

Kyo: low frequency emptiness. Tends towards the reddish in the visible light spectrum.

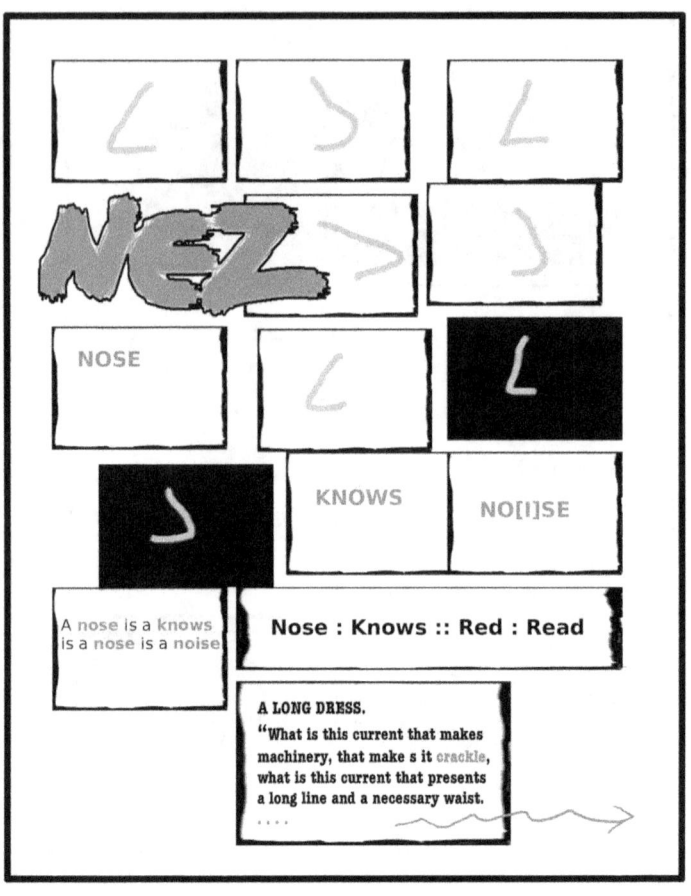

NOSE

KNOWS

NO[I]SE

A nose is a knows is a nose is a noise

Nose : Knows :: Red : Read

A LONG DRESS.

"What is this current that makes machinery, that make s it crackle, what is this current that presents a long line and a necessary waist. . . . .

13

A Rat's Tale of Life in the Wrinkles

I will get to my story of the tall woman's return to the Path but I first want to tell of my slow *jiwa jiwa* through the Hole and my convalescence. I will use aspects of my personal articulation modus of feelings, states, actions, and things as sound words because often there is no other means of expression suitable. A young GenTel, crossbred with ultrasonic hearing for a military career, once coded me in something very close to my own speak after a semi-public rehearsal when I was still juvenile. I was in mediocre voice that day. I heard, or thought I heard, a response wafting through a ventilation duct: *Chuu Chuu, potsun nee. U wai wai alzop eeeee do man ga. Do man ga.* I understood the message to be:

"YOU AM [SIC] NOT ALONE. YOU SING AS THE MAN GOES TO DO. DO IT."

I didn't know then and don't know now what to make of this cryptogram. It could imply that we rats have developed phonetics similar to a graphic form in a human comic tradition called "Manga." I have eaten these colorful words from the newsstand debris on occasion. But I digress ...

As the blue ones disappeared into the vanishing point of my perspectival view that day, I stumbled my way to the sideboard as quickly as I could manage. Still gasping for air through my damaged tracheal apparatus, I dreaded the arrival of a uniform to swat my *pura pura* from this life, incinerate my remains in the enormous fire container in the outside eating area where we often find a plentiful stockpile of rotting tidbits. *Moku archai.* I was aware of my exaggerated *fura yora,* not so different from my awkward posture during a *tsura* on the Path. I could feel the tremble of my hands and feet as I slowly progressed towards the Hole. I conjured a cloud of invisibility around my body to protect me. *Koso.* The terrifying *tsun nuuu* scent of **PC** pet Blue Billy in the Box, lingered in my perfectly functioning snout. He, Billy, ignored my own odor that day, remaining demurely, inexplicably, silent. Perhaps he smelled death without resistance and it bored him.

How long this *jiwa jiwa* took me I cannot say but I was beyond exhaustion when I reached the entrance to the Hole. Few of my clan use this route as its proximity to the Path holds little interest for most, my cousin and I aside. Once through the ass-tight cavity I could follow any one of a dozen burrows to the comfort of my own favorite nest, my Castle Keep, the chamber in the labyrinth that is my crib, my cell, my homey home. I've gouged out several smaller chambers for food storage and evasion, as one must anticipate all types of intruder. We rats favor a single chamber in which to stretch and huddle our weariness from the light and sparkle of the Upper World,

its marvels a mixed bag. As with many species I have encountered, a personal Inside is necessary to deflect the
never-ever-over assault of the spectacular Outside, the
always-on chaosmos. In any case, in the aftermath of the
Path encounter, the need for a quiet space had never felt
more necessary.

Safely composed in my nest I began to lick my wounds.
Vigorously, incessantly, *dondon*. As my tongue is a well-
honed athletic muscle, the enunciator of my vocal utterances, I've developed several techniques for this. There
is *bero bero,* an aggressive licking action recommended
for serious wounds, bacterial illness and post-traumatic stress. *Pero pero,* a softer more sensuous comforting
stroke, wet with memories of my mother's sweet tongue
on my gritty fur, follows.

Once I'd completed the twice daily healing and cleansing ritual, I would sleep. Deeply. *Doyon.* I would dream,
often finding myself exploring a foreign burrow and
its maze of endless dirty, dimpled cavities or venturing
from room to room in a huge, object strewn Upper World
house. I scamper, I skid. On occasion I float, hands and
feet splayed out like a winged bat, high above the scenic
display of my allusions. I tend to remember the dreams
I don't understand, ones with abstract, nonlinear sto-
rylines that pretend to be full of meaning but have nothing rational to offer. I will try to tell this recurring dream
so it makes some sense but of course it will not:

*Folds. Everywhere there are lush doublings of every type to
scamper across and through. The windows on the ground floor
serve as an entrance hole to this two-story architecture that is
home to someone not present. Soft winds and animals such as
myself rush through these openings from the outer milieu, teas-
ing the interior things into new forms. Curtains both velvety
thick and diaphanously transparent rearrange their drape. All*

is in motion, sasa. Bits of loose paper, wadded, marked, and creased are pushed by my ample snout around the parquet floor. Puffed, puu, and pliant pillows are reshaped by the weight of my diving body. Textures. Folds. Fun. Material reality. I entertain the thought that as an outsider in this place, I exert a force upon it, even of the most Pikachu insubstantial kind. I shift the position of a dustball, crumple a curtain crease, drop a shit pile in the corner. I'm a parasite in the host center of a cyclone.

Adventure gets the better of my instincts and I hazard forward via the steep accordion fold of a mahogany staircase, working my way towards the windowless upper floor. Once in this chamber, I experience the ineffable. I'm lucidly aware of my dreaming yet it's still extraordinary. An experience of unpredictable variability assails my presence with the force of an oncoming wave. The intensity of a folding continuum pushes through me. Needing a visual to anchor the spin, I thrillingly recall the glossy image of a big blue wave I sat on in a garbage heap somewhere. I cruise the feeling, maintaining my balance with more prowess than I ever managed in a skid. Hallucinations can be very forgiving. Part water rat, part wet t-shirt in a washing machine spin cycle, I ride it well, screaming an exuberant Aiiiii! as I move through and with other force fields far greater than my own.

Exhausted by the exertion I stop to breathe deeply, claws sunk in the sway of a textured curtain. My relaxation doesn't last long. Eyes wide shut I again witness the specter of a tsunami of great height and strength hovering in suspension above my body in freeze frame. This force, once unleashed, is impossible to fight or ride.

I wait for the water to break.

The urgent twitch of a bursting bladder abruptly aborts the dream. Relieving myself, I recognize the labyrinthine comfort of my burrow with its low ceiling and contoured walls, its claustrophobic coziness, in blatant contrast to my somni-fantasy of the Outside. Tumbling between these realities makes me woozy. I often wish I could control the sensations of my not-yet conscious state as much as I savor the surprise of the uncontrollable. As I recover my strength post-trauma, these images recur in one form or another in nearly every sleep cycle. Like the wave itself, I experience again and again a rolling cartoonish dreamscape fraught with dramatic ups and downs. Still vivid, I remember longing for an unopened package of fluffy marshmallow balls while in the thrall of suspense. I recall the flight line skewered through an incongruous hole in the exposed beam ceiling far above my head, illuminating the foamy crest of the hovering waveform. I cling to this light hole as an anchor in a turbulent topology. I guess this is a tendency of mine. Clinging for dear life to tethers when awash in too much motion; when in a precarious state of balance between an inside that is outside that is inside. This being between, hugging fast to a line that is the porous membrane between worlds, is hard work. It's *shiwa shiwa* – Life in the Wrinkles.

14

Soundings

As B⊗B convalesced he would say *"Kotsu kotsu jiwa,"* aloud to the ants, to the termites, to the profusion of fungal growths carpeting the remnants of his edibles arsenal. He also had several favorite mantras in his wellness arsenal.

The laryngeal area of his body remained sore and contracted even as he regained strength and his appetite returned. Nested away in the privacy of his burrow he worried, incessantly scratching symmetrical dirt pockets in the long tendrils of his lair. Busywork. He hadn't revisited the Path since the spontaneous concert for the tall woman exacted what remained of his strength.

Daily exercise of his delicate vibrators had gradually improved the bandwidth and timbre of his sounding. Like a pubescent male, he lacked control and would often dip two octaves unexpectedly. Disconcerted, he nonetheless carried on as he bore the weight of responsibility to his tribe as their numero uno aesthetic diversion. This brought him little comfort. Post-event, his celebrity status was enhanced by gossip and misinformation but he had little desire to exploit the attention-getting role of wounded hero. He felt himself a hapless perpetrator. Intertwining persistence with denial, he threw himself into his sonification exercises. Besides a practiced ability to hold his alcohol, this is all he knew he knew. The rest was pure instinct.

Confined to his burrow, he had lost track of sunrises and sunsets as temporal markers. Restlessly waking from his recurring tsunami dream, he felt it was time to go forth and visit the Path for a try-out. Time to test the agility of his vocal folds. He hoped she would be present to hear his performance. This is how it had to play out. Sounding and listening needed to be in reciprocity. It mattered. Without her witness to his effort he would be as the sound of one hand clapping.

The route to the Path was forged in his habitual muscle memory. Once through the burrowed labyrinth and the Hole in the storage room, he spotted his cousin passed out in a wet rag on the bottom shelf. He relished the normalcy of this sighting. It was a good omen. Must be a full moon.

Entering the Path he bypassed an urge to skid and rather crept safely along the shadowed plinth of the long corridor. He had chosen his moment well. It was dawn. The place was empty. As in his dreamhouse, here too was one streak of brilliance emanating from a circular skylight in the raftered ceiling. His realities were folding. She was near. Not here but present. He knew she too was wrinkling, as he was.

Steadying his nerves like a talent show contestant, B⊗B opened his throat. Softly at first, then with mounting confidence, he pushed out sound on a long exhale. The waves that massaged his cochlea, bounced from the building's curvilinear surfaces, enveloping this place. The complex overtones were so granularly detuned that their differencing triggered a flurry of aberrant oscillations. Multiple kinetic isotopic reactions vibrated at subatomic levels cleaving bits one from the other. Matter rearranged. The cavernous skidspace was othering. Though the perceivable effects of the rampant quarky shuffling was subtle, the tubular fire extinguisher in the middle of the Path, apparently vulnerable to peculiar phase modulations, began to pucker. Its redness dripped on the slick slick. The strains of *Puru, furu, puru, furi Biiii!* echoed erratically throughout the POMOC. The world was trembling, ionizing, reconfiguring. He knew the shadow lady of the brilliant shoes heard him, felt him.

15

Interview with ShazDada, Part Two

An excerpt from a longer podcast interview which took place in the living room of Bette B, recorded by ShazDada.

SD: [...] I see. Fascinating. Thank you for updating us on the medical research underway as we speak. The possibility of aggressive trans-species genetic mutation is of course almost too incredible to consider yet here we are. I can say this honestly, I think, for everyone following your story, that it's a relief the virus is believed to be non-contagious between humans. Not that we wish you to suffer this alone but, you know, it makes a face-to-face interview a lot easier [both laugh]. And thank you again for letting me speak with you in your home. It's very cozy here. Lots of recycled furniture rather than the molded synthetics I often see in artist's homes. [pause, clears throat] So, it's been a few months now since you encountered B⊘B, as you call him?

BB: Yeah, that's correct. I've lost track of time.

SD: So ... I noticed in our email correspondence that you write B⊘B with capital B's and a slashed O ... what do you call that symbol anyway?

BB: I don't know really. It's the international symbol for not-doing. DO NOT … ! I have my own name for it. I call it a "NOT or better NAUGHT." [giggling] Equal parts danger and void. It's edgy don't you think? I can get lost in the nothingness of that queer-zero placeholder between the Bs. It's just a fetish I guess. For some it's shoes, for me it's palindromes.

SD: So it's symbolic? Is it a scientific reference or a literary reference? Or maybe a spiritual reference?

BB: I don't know, I just find it, uhm, yeah, appropriate somehow. I'm really not sure why. Perhaps I do him an injustice to name him, anthropomorphize him, but well, I, uhm, allow myself this indiscretion. I guess it's a sign of weak personal politics. But now that we speak of it … I was talking about him to a friend of mine and she immediately associated the name with Bølle Bob, an iconic bad boy in Danish children's culture. There's a catchy, kitschy tune the kids all sing apparently. [singing]

Bob Bob Bølle Bob, Bølle Bob Bob.

Bob Bob Bølle Bob, Bølle Bob Bob.

Sticks with you as a nasty little earworm. But I'm wandering a bit here and still do want to address, as I mentioned last time, well I do want to speak about ethics … yeah … so can I do that now? Or would you like me to keep singing? [both laugh]

SD: Please, yes, let's move to the topic of ethics and human relations with the nonhuman.

BB: OK. So I was recently reading a critical essay by a post-humanist scholar, I forget his name, Clark somebody, anyway it was on Levinas, you know Emmanuel Levinas, the French philosopher of ethics?

SD: I'm not familiar with him.

BB: Do you want to hear this side story?

SD: Sure, if you think it's relevant to our audience.

BB: I can never be sure anything I have to say is of interest but I'll keep it short [shuffles papers] ... here it is ... it's only three pages.

SD: Great. I'm sure you can translate the philosophical jargon for our listeners.

BB: I'll do my best. So, Levinas writes on his experiences as a prisoner in a Nazi labor camp during WWII. He tells of a dog the captives named "Bobby" and how this animal would greet them every day as they traipsed back and forth from their "day jobs" with a happy bark and wagging tail. "Bobby" was the only living organism in that camp, in that town, that treated the prisoners as human, offered them some residual feeling of existence with his friendly, daily acknowledgement. The point is that even this being the case, Levinas could not grant an inclusive ethical status to any being not human, even this sentient, affectionate dog. It's a disappointing argument in an otherwise credible body of thought though I have to be upfront and admit I haven't studied him much.

SD: So you disagree with Levinas?

BB: Yeah, I do. To deny animals, even plants a place at the ethical table is problematic. Maybe that's the ground zero of the problem. The Table. The *food* on the table I mean. You know, "we are what we don't eat" kinda thing.

Anyway, in this century we're much more comfortable collapsing the hierarchical status of the human species. Epicurus was a precursor of this kind of cosmo thinking as was Whitehead, Alfred, but I won't go into that now. Remember I told you last time I like him. And of course Isabelle...

SD: Right. I suppose this gives our listeners some insight into your views on animal rights.

BB: Well, there's much more to say, it's a knotty issue, but the analogy of would-be lab rat B⊗B and Bobby the undeserving dog is worth pointing out which is why I mentioned it.

SD: Returning to your story ... how have you been spending your time the past few weeks? It's apparent now that you're undergoing some striking changes to the human phenotype and I wonder, all my readers and listeners are wondering, how you're handling this transformation? I must say you seem to be coping rather well.

BB: Let's say I'm handling it. I'm seeing several therapists. One is a GenTel psychologist with ultrasonic hearing capability. He's helping me control the noise factor. The excess bandwidth of my hearing alone could drive any sane person to distraction. He's teaching me how to AD. That means a-tune and d-stress. That's how he puts it. I must learn to selectively filter ambient noise – white, pink, brown – all the squeaks, squawks, and buzz of organic and inorganic worlds. I need to zoom in and out of sonic chaos with some semblance of acuity. I see your recorder is a *Zooom*, a zippy name but a misnomer. It can't do that ... zoom ... Anyway, there's an exaggerated spatiality to my hearing now. I've been intrigued by the Pythagorean notion of the music of the spheres. It's been long discredited you know, but if you reboot the theory as vibrations of subatomic strings it gets interesting again. I haven't yet learned to clearly distinguish between vibrational sources so I can't say much more about this yet. My ears are still swimming in an undefined soup of sensation. Yet in some perverse way, it's kinda liberating, being so detached from meaning.

SD: OK but ooops [pen dropping to floor] ... let's pursue it a bit more in depth before we move on to other adaptations you're going through. It would seem that the increased auditory sensitivity and your developing sense of smell has upended your everyday coping mechanisms of living in the world. Is that true?

BB: Yes, I haven't the temperament or stamina to deal with anything other than the sensational right now. My "team" ... the biologists, geneticists, oncologists, internists, epidemiologists, ethologists, psychologists, blah, blah ... assigned to my case are baffled by the speed at which my cells are reorganizing and adapting to the parasite or parasites I'm hosting. They haven't yet identified them. Apparently I'm one of the more interesting forensic mysteries of the century thus far. Or so they all tell me in an encouraging kind of way. You know, the "You go girl!" kinda talk. But I had to put a limit on the weekly prodding, poking, and scanning at the clinic. My body, my spirit, my psychological disposition are thoroughly done in. I long for the comfort of my own home, burrowing beneath the solace of the bedcovers, hiding from the feeding frenzy of ambitious scientists, bloggers, and the tabloid press. Yourself excluded of course.

SD: Well, thanks for being so candid about your experiences with me and allowing me inside the privacy of your home. But could we stay on topic for a minute. Back to the alterations in your sense of hearing ... You mentioned in a tweet that you can now distinguish frequencies up to

±50 kHz? I did a bit of research on this … My, that's seriously denting the ultrasonic bandwidth. What's it like to hear that high? It must be painful. Actually it's unfathomable that you're able to remain sane.

BB: As I said, one adjusts, learns to filter, much like the way we all shut out ambient noise when we're chatting at a café. There's just a lot more to attend to. As I said, it's exhausting. All the raw, edgy newness, that's what gets to me … all these sounds I've never before registered. I need to somehow archive and map them as sensations but there is a seeming infinity of soundings and with enhanced hearing you become hyper-aware of, how can I say this without … well, do you know about the theory of the multiverse?

SD: Uhm, I think so. It's speculative physics, like string theory's eleven dimensions right? Or what is it, quantum field theory and super symmetry? Something like that … and the multiverse idea posits that we're having this conversation in a billion other world bubbles, each with different rules of physics and maybe in one you're a man or a rat and I'm wearing blue instead of red and so on.

BB: Yes! [excited] That's basically it without the math. I don't understand the math either. [laughing] Anyway, I have this feeling, and I know it sounds totally crazy, but sometimes I think I am listening in on parallel worlds. It's hard to explain, but imagine simultaneous repetition. This layered or superpositioned finely nuanced difference. It's a thickening feeling yet somehow elastic. Thickening, not sickening, though now that I say it this way I realize I am often viscerally affected. I puke a lot these days but it feels like a cleansing mechanism. Anyway, I'm partial to the multiverse theory because I think I hear it. Sometimes I think I smell it. Anyway, wrapping myself in thick, or maybe folded is a better term, folded multiplicities of reality somehow grounds me. Undergrounds me. Like feeling tremors in the safety of a deep hole. [pause; clears throat] But you probably want to know about the singing right? Actually, it's also very difficult to describe.

SD: [loud exhale] Phew. This is quite a lot to consider but yes, I was coming to the singing of course.

BB: OK. I don't understand yet what, why or how I'm privy to what I now hear, the multiverse theory aside. The geneticists working with me think I am biologically attuned, via some accelerated DNA quirk, to the frequencies of the Rodentia species and that's why I pick up on specific tonal patterns. [chair squeaking] So yeah, the best way to explain the sensation of the singing is that it sounds like birdsong but it's weirdly more guttural even though the intonation is stratospherically high. The experience of the song, well I've only ever heard B⊗B, as far as I know, but it exceeds any possibility of describing it with uhm, language. I'm hearing some kind of plaintive cosmic tune and at the same time my guts are rattling. Rattling! Ha! That's a good word.

SD: Rattling? You mean you feel a trans-species sensation of coming undone?

BB: Whoa. Good one Shaz! But ... not really undone ... more like a corporeal modulation with emotional qualities. And, once, I swear I heard this, there were two voices. Not in a call and response ritual like mating birds, but in a duet. Like the technique Buddhist monks practice. It was extraordinary. Two parallel lines, one higher and more expressive, more vibrato so to speak, the other like a droning, supportive harmony with less pitch variation. Anyway, it's not comparable to our familiar calibration of sympathetic vibrations but it's not not like that either. It's a very specific example simultaneous repetitions or parallel worlds I was talking about before. But different. As I said, words fail me again ... rattling ... I like that ... rattled. I'm rattled. God, I wish I didn't like puns so much. [laughing]

SD: Maybe this is a good moment to move on to a discussion of what most of my readers and listeners are keen to learn more about, what can we call it ... your morphological transformation.

BB: Uh huh, yes. What would you like to know?

SD: Ah, well, as much as you're willing to tell. I don't want to trap you into a corner with inappropriate questions. Hmmm, maybe that's an awkward way of putting it. [water pouring; water spilling to floor] I see you're still wearing the kinky red latex gloves. [both laugh] Perhaps you could tell us about your daily routines and about, how did you call it last time – Tattarrattat – the Joycean wake-up call that sits on your left cheek? About the changes to your skin surfaces, the shape of your nose ...

BB: I can address these things.

SD: Great. We are aware your condition is altogether inexplicable by any contemporary biological or medical categorization. You are amazing and mystifying scientists and philosophers from every conceivable specialization. That said, a handful of artists are on the beat, as it were, with the remarkable event your evolving condition presents. I've seen some interesting work popping up lately in performance galleries and downtown graffiti. Have you seen the rat silhouette's that line the sidewalks near the bakeries and vegan franchises? Brilliant. But, the provocation is clear and I want to leave the storytelling to you.

BB: Could we take a small break first? I need to freshen my hands as I have this uhm, medicinal routine. It will help me to, uhm, collect my thoughts.

SD: Surely.

[seven-minute break]

SD: [tapping mic] We're back with Bette B and the ongoing saga of her extraordinary transformation.

BB: Yes. The changes. My *jiwa jiwa*. There are new names for things in my world, neologisms just kinda pop to mind. I feel them as phonetic utterances as I can't find ready descriptors for the flux state of my becoming-whatever. These sounds appear randomly purposeful so I use them. Am I too esoteric here about these sensually and nonsensually perceived occurrences?

SD: No, no, well ... nonsensually ... ? No just go on ...

BB: OK, so microperceptions seem to percolate and perish in what feels like an expanding middle, my *potsun hara hara* I call it. I have real problems with recognition yet I'm somehow navigating with an explorer's excitement and lack of trepidation. I was never particularly courageous before, even afraid of my own shadow after midnight, so this is all pretty strange.

SD: And how are you adjusting to your celebrity status?

BB: Ha! I call it *shiiin* – the sound of silent staring. It has a fluctuating frequency within the human range, in fact it's very low, subwoofer low, around 40 Hz. It's everywhere I go. I've gotten used to it and, to be honest, it's a calming antidote to the ultrasonic vibrations. Almost everything has a sound now – love, stars, wrinkles, blushing, anger, sadness, smoothness – it's a language I'm learning.

SD: Can you give us an example of what you hear now?

BB: Sure. [clearing throat] *Hiiie, Piii! Puru furu, furi. Biiii, Buwa! Chun, pari. Chi chi, chirin. Kiiiii!* [microphone feedback]

SD: My ...

BB: Sorry, I can get a bit carried away.

SD: What is it exactly you're singing? Is it singing ... ? Or ... You appear to be transported.

BB: Really, I have no idea but I've heard these sounds before, they come from B⊗B, I'm sure of that, and I repeat them. I'm really not very original.

SD: Fascinating. [water pouring] Could you maybe say something about the changes to your nose, your enhanced scenting abilities?

BB: OK. The enhancements to my sense of smell have come more slowly, they're evolving at a different speed. Scentsing. Right now it's more uncomfortable and disturbing than my overzealous hearing. There is so much *tsun tsun* I never noticed before. I can hardly breathe sometimes. I have a strange love/hate relationship with decay now. Rot is the worst smell and the most seductive smell. It's weird mix, a Vanitas *memento mori* of the sumptuous and the dying in one whiff. Everything has a scentuous decay factor. Food, furniture, feces, fungus, feet, functions, fog, fictives, fortitude, fucking. [pause] What a string of "F" words. Funny that. Anyway, I respect the decaying process and find entropy naturally beautiful but the smell of it is less than fine. It's just like the sound of smiling I was talking about. Just like sound, all things and non-things seem to have a scent. So, here I go again with ... [pause] I kinda like the ad nauseam flow of lists ... anyway ... stars, friendship, mountains, thought, shining, blushing, anger, shock, happiness. Like that. They *sound*. And for me, sound and smell entangle in a cacophony of sensory data that, well you'd think it would overload my central nervous system but somehow, perceptually, I cope. My survival mechanisms are strong and getting stronger. [glass rattles, sipping water]

SD: This is all very difficult for us to imagine. It's so ... so extraordinary, what's happening to you.

BB: I have techniques. Yoga's good. Meditation is tricky coz the sensations amplify. It's like sitting on a cushioned knife edge between nothing and too much. I read philosophy, French mostly. You know, contemporary process-oriented stuff.

SD: Hmmm. I never thought it could actually be useful. So, aah, do you have any other means of relaxation?

BB: My taste for wine is slowly decreasing but there's, uhm, the Purello. I've developed a ritual technique, a way of licking the stuff *bero bero* from my hands and forearms. Have you ever taken hallucinogens?

SD: No.

BB: Well, to be honest I only experimented in college and that was ages ago, but it's that kind of high. Very much like a dream state. Ironically, the stuff that supposedly keeps me in a non-contaminate state is the same stuff that helps me feel my potential. Or, I can say this better ... unfolds the abstract as the real it is.

SD: Hmmm, and how do feel about the more visible changes, the ones that produce, as I understand it, the ubiquitous, encompassing sound of *shiiin,* the sound of staring? Tattarrattat, the shifting registers in your voice, the subtle widening of your nostrils, the thickening hair on your limbs, though I don't see that now ... ? These physically visible attributes must be disconcerting?

BB: I have been frequenting my local wax bar. The attendants are adjusting to what we now call the "Hirsute Global" as opposed to the Brazilian. [loud laughing] Hurts like hell but I sometimes need to reconnect to human prescriptions for normalcy. My voice isn't a major problem as of yet though I sense it altering, somehow diminishing even though I'm convinced I can speak outside the frame of human hearing. It's a strange paradoxical feeling.

SD: And RatTat?

BB: Yes, the *gira*glowing gift from B⊗B's own hands that is the source of all my dismay. Situated on my cheek as it is, it exhibits my moods in a wildly extrovert fashion. You can't believe how many people approach me about it.

SD: There's a recent cheeky gif from an artist called GlowTat that has gone, ahhh ... viral. [loud laughing]

BB: Yeah I saw it! The hysterical strobo blinking one with the soylent green frogs and the hoops right?

SD: Yeah. [still laughing] And those vibrating prismatic guerilla gorilla masks. Wild!

BB: Well, as I used to say, "Immanence trumps Transcendence." [sound of water glass placed on table] Do you get that?

SD: No, not really.

BB: That's OK, I don't say it any more. Like that.

[end of excerpt]

16

Blue Betty and Bob

"There's a plastic juice bottle crumpled under the left wheel. Get it out of there so we can move dammit."

"Hold your goddamn horses Betty, I've got to find a stick or something to poke it."

"We've got ten different kinds of prodders in the box marked 'Prodders' idiot. Just use one of them. Try the three footer with the talon tip."

"OK. Wait a sec while I find it ... Got it! Why do you always use animal metaphors for everything? It's fucking unoriginal. OK. Wiggle the wagon just a little to help me dislodge this thing. Yeah. That's it. A little more ... a little more. Now give the front wheels a good jerk. Got it!"

"All that commotion. You woke Billy up and he's a pisser when he's jostled."

[Loud barking from a box buried underneath a double gas burner camping stove and a paper mâché model of Mount Vesuvius found in a dumpster outside the Geographic Museum that Bob holds dear for some inexplicable reason.]

"Shut the fuck up Billy or I'll smack ya one. We're mobile again, dammit."

"Where to Mrs.? Shall we get a 'bird's eye view' of the station from the mezzanine?"

"You're really annoying you know that. And I don't give a rat's ass about animal metaphors ... Let's have lunch by the PostOffice incinerator. It's warm over there and we might get lucky today. I got a hunch it's a better location than the Q line."

"Anything you say Madame. The world is your oyster."

"Cut the crap Bob and push a bit harder, you always make me do most of the heavy work."

"What would you do without me Bets? I'm the one that plays the pipes so good and sweet. You'd probably starve without my trillin'. Billy aside, my breath and spit swirling in these holey tubes is still our most effective weapon."

"Is that your qualitative or quantitative assessment?"

"Bit of both I reckon."

"Hmmph. PUSH for god's sake."

[Barking from the box subsides to a lazy growl as the steel casters on the luggage cart rhythmically clank along the refurbished brick walkways of City's downtown.]

17

Blue Marble

Waiting for something to happen, Bette B pulls a dusty copy of Montaigne's *Collected Essays* from the shelf. First published in the late sixteenth century as literary "try outs," these musings, some brief, some extensive, made a long-term impact on the way of the written word, kicking off a new style of skeptical pondering. It's her lure of the day, exerting a pull like iron filings to a rare earth magnet. The spine cracks as she randomly opens to "On Idleness." Long ago, she'd marked the page in pencil, underlining words and scribbling marginalia:

> When lately I retired to my house resolved that, in so far as I could, I would cease to concern myself with anything except the passing in rest and retirement of the little time I still have to live, <u>I could do my mind no better service than to leave it in complete idleness</u> to commune with itself, to come to rest, and to grow settled; which I hoped it would thenceforth be able to do more easily, since it had become graver and more mature with time. But I find,
>
> *variam semper dant otia mentem,*
>
> that, on the contrary, like a <u>runaway horse,</u> it is a hundred times more active on its own behalf than ever it was for others. It presents me with so many <u>chimeras and imaginary monsters</u>, one after another, <u>without order or plan</u>, that, in order to contemplate their oddness

and absurdity at leisure, <u>I have begun to record them in writing</u>, hoping in time to make my mind ashamed of them.

Surprised by the emphasized reference to chimeras, horses, monsters, and the need to record the absurdities of daily thought, she perks up. Surely this is random browsing at its most effective. Absently grabbing the chipped handle of her cadmium yellow ceramic mug in a flush of excitement, she's disappointed to find coffee dregs. Making a second cup, she prepares for a bout of intense reading before shifting into writing mode.

Pre-incident, Bette B had been exploring the relation between two broad conceptual themes, the "monstrous" and the "holey." Her research had produced some stimulating connections. She had been crafting a text, commissioned by an online art journal, with the working title "Precarity and the Monstrous Void." Post-incident, this subject has taken on a titillating prophetic character. Lurking deep in the holes of the free market derivative, in the *objet d'art,* in the blow-up sex toy, in the bearded lady, in the elephant man, lay a balm to her unrest. Rhythmically scratching her left forearm, she realizes she must plumb the "concept" as an antidote to her troubles; assuage her somatic anxiety with speculative froth as potent as the ethyl alcohol she immoderately consumes. She must draw a diagram. Connect the dots. She is, after all, an odd duck. An unhinged specimen. Certainly, in all her inglorious singularity she must address a monstrosity's response-ability. But to whom? To an incomprehensible Society? To a nebulous Culture? To a fascist Politic? To a dying Earth? She'd read somewhere that contextualizing an impersonal Planet enabled a framing of "the world without us." She settles then on the Blue Marble as the matter of her concern, remembering in after thought the day she stole the Fall 1968 Whole Earth Catalog from a new titles display.

But how might her essay now play out? She is a horse run wild, clomping over a vast landscape of sodden field and lush terrain, pitched against the granular boundary of shifting sand and flowing waters. She licks and glows, listens and sniffs within the measure of her small apartment that is, as in her dreams, ever expanding and accumulating room after new room. Becoming monster, she breathes the collective air, inhaling and exhaling molecules passed through countless generations of animals and plants. Oxygen works its dualistic magic as life gas and toxic waste, again and again.

Emptying her second cup of coffee, she curiously recalls a dream jotted down before the holidays. Opening her journal to her own essayistic scribble, she rereads her account of 10 December's nocturnal happening.

A newly discovered Euripidian fragment on the flight of Icarus was generating a slew of derivative theater. One such script had been granted generous production funds from the otherwise stingy cultural pot the entrenched neoliberal government had allotted the arts. Theater in particular was suffering the blow of devastating cutbacks. "Spawn of Daedalus" was set to premier in a few months time. The classical theme apparently appealed to both aesthetes and politicians as each could identify with the fallen ambitions of the central protagonist.

Chosen to direct the work, I decided the play, a monologue for Icarus, would be acted in parallel readings, one taking place in a white, claustrophobic cubic space, mounted on the stage with only one sightline from the central king's position. An audience of 15 would sit in a neat single row on a steeply raked tribune facing the open façade of the tiny tomb room. The performer would recite the original script, translated to English by Grigorios T.

The performer, an athletic non-actor would purposefully strug-
gle with it. I had signed David Beckham to the role due to his
convincing underwear ad.

A parallel production was to take place simultaneously on the
roof of the theater. Triangulated cameras would project the
action to the audience below. A 15 cm thick natural fiber sail-
ing rope would be hung from the roof to the stage floor like a
plumb line, connecting the dramatic spaces. Atop, Imelda Mar-
cos would play Icarus in Anne Carson's automatic writing "re-
sponse" to the unearthed play. Creating the gaping hole in the
theater roof, through the complex lighting grid and structural
maze of rafters would present the single biggest technical prob-
lem. This was the least of my directorial worries. An image for
the promotional poster appeared with intense clarity.

18

Forensic Clues

She was drifting, losing the thread of her impulse. The Purello does that. She refocused. "Monsters. Where are the monsters?" Returning to her bookcase she spots her target, nestled alongside a first edition of John Gardner's *Grendel*. On occasion, there was method in her archival madness. Pulling out a book of Derrida interviews, she checks the index for keywords and finds a scrolling list of "monster" citings. The first entry reveals this:

Monsters cannot be announced. One cannot say: "Here are our monsters," without immediately turning the monsters into pets.

Were Montaigne's self-described monstrous imaginings, once out of the pen, so to speak, now domesticated pink-eyed albino bunnies of the tamest sort? Like GenTel hybrids or virtually any breed of "man's best friend"? She's quibbling but it's of importance to her as she fancies herself, on good days, the anticipated arrivant. Or doth she think too lustrously of her predicament? She searches for another interview fragment, imagining an older Frenchman and an earnest academic sitting at a café in Paris or Berlin, sipping strong coffee with a clunky tape recorder placed conspicuously on a small, scarred table littered with cigarette ash.

JD: [...] But the notion of the monster is rather difficult to deal with, to get a hold on, to stabilize. A monster may be obviously a composite figure of heterogeneous organisms that are grafted onto each other. This graft, this hybridisation, this composition that puts heterogeneous bodies together may be called a monster [...] monstrosity may reveal or make one aware of what normality is.

Bette B can't help thinking of the description of inoculation she looked into some weeks ago as she was being initiated to life as a specimen. "To graft in or implant the germs of a disease as into the bud of a plant, or into the skin of a victim." She considers for a moment the implications of the graft itself as monstrous. Too old to be GenTel, she has not had to confront the efficacy of her chromosomal origins as many of her students have. This Frankensteinian complicity excites her fantasy. She nearly drifts off into another ethanol-driven episode of sublime supposition but instead, deftly reels in the whip of her casting line to continue reading:

JD: But a monster is not just that, it is not just this chimerical figure in some way that grafts one animal onto another, one living being onto another. A monster is always alive, let us not forget.

Yes, Yes. She's agitated now, on her feet. Ridiculously, she craves a Camel as she prances through her apartment, disappointed in the knee-jerk reaction since she quit smoking fifteen years ago. Clues. Lots of clues! Derrida was emitting a post-mortem stream of evidence as forensically potent as a DNA sample. Philosophers, the clever ones slightly off the grid, were at heart detectives. Not so much interested in determining truths as adrenalized by the chase, attending to the unfamiliar, the unknown.

JD: Simply, it shows itself [*elle se montre*] — that is what the word monster means — it shows itself in something that is not yet shown and that therefore looks like a hallucination, it strikes the eye, it

frightens precisely because no anticipation had prepared one to
identify this figure [...]

Such a delicious word, "hallucination." It can be read as
synonymous with "epiphany" if the conditions are favorable, when the clues converge in a PAAF! or a BOOM!
or an AHA! Closing her eyes she recalls that elusive instant in the Corridor when *Rattus norvegicus* became *Cavia
porcellus* in the grip of her own wooly, mittened hands.
She aborts the thought as the violent memory intensifies.
Reading further:

JD: [...] as soon as one perceives a monster in a monster, one begins
to domesticate it ...

Her skeletal frame is vibrating like a tuning fork, pulsing
a frequency even her evolving ears cannot transduce.

JD: [...] the future is necessarily monstrous: the figure of the future,
that is, that which can only be surprising, that for which we are not
prepared, you see, is heralded by species of monsters.

Bette B rereads the entire interview, her heart pounding against the brittle rib cage that protects this delicate
pump from the rowdy outside. Anxious, thrilled, terrified. Why she thinks of the Dylan line "The pumps don't

work coz the vandals took the handles" as she attempts to steady her pulse is beyond even her copious gift of bizarre association. Pulse. Heart. Pump. She nervously plunges the Purello bottle, blind to the obvious connotation. Sucking from her trembling digits while reading, she wonders what to do with this information? Something once abstract is now concrete. And to make matters worse, it's personal.

Lost in quixotic meanderings, she imagines herself walking a domesticated rat on a long leash along the dirt footpaths of Peoples Park and takes weird comfort in the normalcy of her projection, wondering if any of her Twitter followers might dream of taking her own Rat-tatted, rat-addled nee rattled self on a chaperoned walk through public space one day? ShazDada perhaps?

19

Bette B's Tendencies

Night 336

Haven't written in awhile. Nothing to say.

Night 345

*Yesterday the Team began experimenting with techniques to re-
duce the thresholds of my evolving cochlea and olfactory epithe-
lium. They fight amongst themselves about procedures. The otolaryngologist on my case, a well-meaning GenTel, would rather
study my condition than cure it, research the radical phenomena
of my abilities rather than normalize them to human parame-
ters. Though his goals are self-serving, he respects the process of
metamorphosis. I'm literally his pet project and I actually agree
with this medical approach as I've learned quite organically to
cope with an enormous bandwidth of sound and smell. I want
to move forward while facing backward. Angelus Novus and all
that. ZeNeZ, the affable Dark Precursor. I try to tell them, convince them to let me be what I will have become. The head of
the clinic, a card-carrying Harvard asshole, wants to cure me.
To save me from myself. He'll righteously put me through every
painful procedure that experimental chemistry and advanced
prosthetics can conjure up. To keep the monster in check. So the*

lab coats fight amongst themselves. They think I don't know but my nose knows.

Night 350

So here's the kicker. A behind-the-scenes debate is raging. It has to do with my species status. There are ethical standards for medical experimentation on humans, on stem cells, and other-thans. Apparently I now fall in a liminal in-between. "Neither fish nor foul" they keep saying. I'm the biggest damn conundrum of their veritable careers. Fair game or protected species? In any case I'm certainly an ethical trendsetter, perhaps a standard bearer. Thus the overheated disputes, the physical skirmishes and hallway fisticuffs in a morality war I find mildly amusing. As yet, they haven't asked me my feelings on the matter. Typical. I wonder if they've named me "Bobby" behind my back?

Night 356

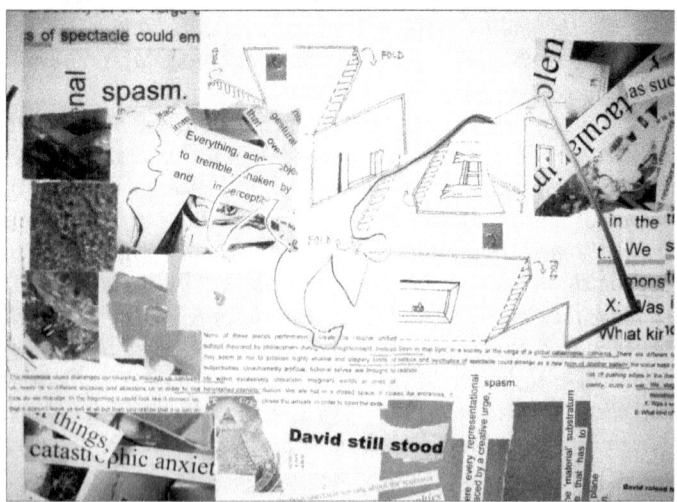

Night 358

In the 17C, the grand epoch of natural philosophy, gentlemen and alchemists would experiment on themselves to gain credibility for their hypotheses. Personal risk-taking was the etiquette of scientific experiment. Isaac Newton famously poked the back of his eye socket with a knitting needle to report on his optical experience of prismatic colors. What would old Isaac make of Rat-Tat I wonder? In an age of disreputable cultural conduct, arguably not greater or lesser than any other century's, this practice stands out as potentially ethically superior to 21C conveyor belt experimentation on rats and bunnies, dogs and monkeys IMHO.

Night 360

I looked into the use of lab rats in studies of presbyphonia when my voice first began to gasp. [Note: As my auditory capacity advances to superhuman levels, my speaking ability retreats]. Breathy, hoarse, the language I'm inventing is catered to augment this deficit. The lazy flutter in my larynx first appeared in lock step with RatTat's glow.

Night 369

Why do I like the letter "Z" so much? Zigzag. ZeNeZ. I think it's because I like to write it. To draw it. I overheard the epidemiologist talking about zoonotic diseases yesterday and naturally my senses tingle. SARS, Lyme Disease, the Black Plague. I'm adding Zombie to my list of favorite "Z" words. The passing of zoonotic infection between humans is of course what they're all pissing in their pants about here. The watch and wait and go home and pray I'm a one-off.

Night 371

I recently declined ShazDada's invitation for a third interview for fear my comments will not be understood. She's coaxing hard but I'm adamant. Writing is a more reliable linguistic form at this stage of my development. And anyway, I've always been embarrassed by the idiomatic content of my spoken statements, my conversational banter peppered with every sort of sophomoric, colloquial, vernacular expression. It's even more complicated now that I uncontrollably slip between tongues. The gap between written language and spoken language, in my case, has always been vast. It's as though I bifurcate into another character entirely depending on the communicative mode of employ. So, I have to say "NO" to a verbal interview.

Night 380

The evangelists seem to be winning the war. They will conserve my humanity even if it kills me.

20

Blue Betty's Monsters

Smothered in malodorous layers of salvaged sheep woolies, Blue Betty, once a chronic insomniac when an up-and-comer yuppie, sleeps in the open urban air as the dead do. Millennial passers-by continue on, phone to ear. Sleep. It's a stunning perk in an otherwise precarious life. Bob, usually nearby, also sleeps deeply but does not, or cannot, enjoy the resilience REM cycles afford. Perhaps his resistance evokes an irreversible hereditary responsibility to stand guard? She really doesn't care, happy that she gets enough night rest to traipse through the next day, pushing the stuff of their conjoined lives on their rolling home like mutant turtles. She's been a certified Pest Controller for two years and is beginning to take a certain pride in her achievements and skills, surprised to encounter satisfaction in the most menial of service professions. Still, she only displays her **PC** badge for strategic purposes.

Wiping crusty ochre sleepdust from the corners of her eyes, she reruns one of last night's many internal flicks. She had always hoped to become a serious a writer, a novelist, an investigative journalist, maybe a librettist. Her Master's degree in Comparative Literature had never helped her professionally advance beyond producing creative advertising copy. Her most memorable yet fleeting success was her campaign for a vegan franchise that played on the '80s "Where's the beef?" slogan with a stupid knock knock joke spin-off.

> Knock knock.
> Where's the Beef?
> On the cow, on the cow!
> (Repeat Chant ...)

An obnoxious mantra, it took on a short-lived earworm status until it naturally faded from advert slot-time, consigned to the compost heap of perishables. Having exhibited limited skills in this field, she was one of the first in her advertising firm to be made redundant in the midst of yet another non-credible financial crisis. Initially, she took the blow with grace. Relishing a bit a freedom from workplace demands, taking time off to travel. Four months of vigorous globetrotting wafted into four years of inertia. Savings exhausted, all prospects soon followed suit. Given her composure during employment interviews was alarmingly unstable, she found herself spinning in a monotonous loop, a mouse in a wheel. Awaiting extinction.

Now wide awake, Betty's latest dalliance with the surreal had triggered the memory of a transparent *Visible Woman* doll she was given on her twelfth birthday from her father. Immobilized for a summer, she was recovering from the bite of a fierce German Shepherd. Two skin graft operations left a scar in the shape of a cumulus cloud on her left calf. Her hip flesh was now forever plastered over her upper soleus muscle. At the time, she thought the medical mannequin an odd gift. Doubtless her father was inspired to direct her trauma towards colorful, mucousfree, plastic organs encased in an expressionless, mature female body. The ironic name of the gutsy educational toy did not escape her notice.

⁜

This morning, crumpled in an exterior corner enclave of a granite hi-rise, warmed by the steamy residue rising from a manhole cover, she wondered about the present state of her entrails. What colors, what shapes, would her eviscerated intestines, her liver, her spleen reveal if exposed to the chilly spring air? The perfectly bloodless Visible Woman meets the imperfectly homeless Invisible Woman. Fate, mektoub, kismet – that causeless meta-effect worshipped by many, is way too fickle for her taste. She prefers to put her betting money on dreams. One day she'll win the Lotto big time. One day she'll grow young and take a long thrilling skid in the Corridor, leaving her trolley and her pathetic husband in the dust. One day she'll fly.

Months ago, in a rare spirit of fairness, Betty'd agreed that Bob could lug around his volcanic model if she could keep her stash of memorabilia. Stretching her cramped legs, she rose this fine morning on the prowl for her favorite useless item. Dexterously she rearranged the dented cardboard boxes on the cart, careful to not rouse the sleeping Billy. Now, right now, she wanted to touch it. Folded away in a box marked "STUFF", buried underneath a packet of old love letters, a feminista "Blonde Betty" button and a faded "Best All Around Girl" ribbon from third grade, lay a bright scarlet unitard and cape, the remnants of a wild, orgiastic costume party two decades ago. She'd once had a pair of matching latex gloves and slippers but had misplaced them. Eyes closed, lightly caressing the synthetic fabric, she grafted wonder woman superpowers onto cellulite flesh.

As her physical strength slowly dissipates, she'll one day be forced to reconsider the value of her belongings solely

on the basis of their material weight and is as yet unde-
cided whether this is disturbing or liberating criteria.

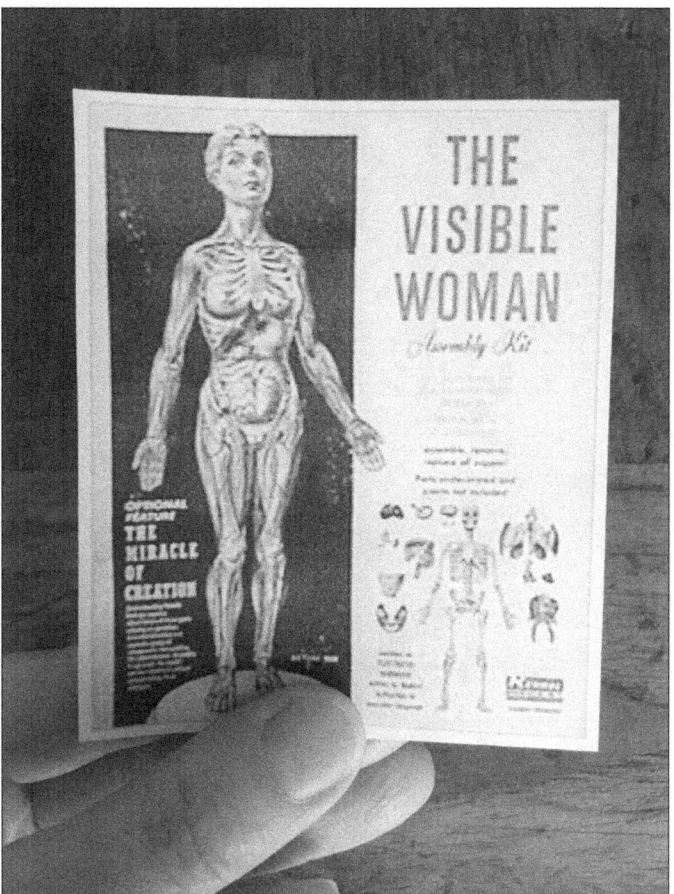

21

Blue Bob's Holes

1. rat
2. sink
3. ass
4. glory
5. whoopie
6. worm
7. rabbit
8. sewer
9. stink
10. moth
11. port
12. peep
13. escape
14. button
15. man
16. mouth
17. doughnut

Volcano.
Nostril.
Gun.
Absence.
Aperture.
Zero.

He thinks of himself as a virtual fly fisher, casting his life-line into the sweeping rush of uncertainty. Hooking holes. A less lofty identification of his being might stem from his daily regimen of stoking prodders into angles and crevices of all sorts in his drowsy search for vermin. It's a too obvious subliminal substitute for the sex he no longer enjoys with Betty, though this thought prompts the question "if" he ever enjoyed sex with Betty? Hard to say when one's libidinous appetite is forever stunted by the stench of urine in a dark alleyway. Conditions were rarely favorable for romance. With nary a word passing between, they had arrived at a mutual cease and desist order from lusty activity. But he's not complaining. After all, he's still got his ace in the hole, that kinky, well-fitting Vesuvius model Betty lets him keep nearby. Works wonders.

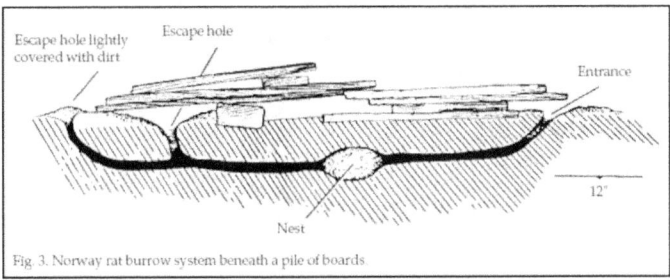

Fig. 3. Norway rat burrow system beneath a pile of boards.

Escape hole lightly covered with dirt

Escape hole

Entrance

12"

Nest

22

Topologies

B⊗B wasn't sleeping well lately. If he managed to doze off his dreams would wake him. He'd been anxious and couldn't quite grasp why. His voice, different, was fit in a fresh way. Dazzling even, if one had ears for the experimentally unpretty. He couldn't help but notice that he now had a younger following of walkabout rats with an adventurous taste in soundings. He enjoyed the revival of his status though the praise he garnered was often for his epic recuperative efforts. Publically he was flourishing. Privately he was unhinged.

Adjusting to the effects of rabid insomnia was a matter of real concern. This, he reckoned, was the one annoying fly in the ointment of his total recovery. Prior to his encounter with the woman on the Path he had gone about his daily activities in an habitual mode: sleep, dream, wake, fuck, gather foodstuffs, fuck, eat copiously, lick, fuck, eat again, lick again, skid (depending on conditions), lick, sleep, hallucinate ... Begin again. Just as day and night conflate in the recesses of his burrow, his dream actions neatly fold into his waking wanderings. His dream state experiences used to be every bit as bold as his hyper-sensory awareness while out and about. The incident on the Path and its subsequent effects had momentarily brought the pervasiveness of multiple realities to his attention.

Now, with perpetual lack of sleep, he was thoroughly dull around the edges, often dangerously pushing his exertions beyond the limits of his fatigue. The irregular fits and starts of his somni-being were tangibly diminishing his experience of the Outside. As he hoped for an average-to-long life span this weakened intensity was worrying. It did not bode well.

⁂

Rattus norvegicus are notorious neophobes. Novelty is threatening, though this effect is easily overcome as suspicion of the new gets old fast.

Habitual practice has proved throughout millennia to be a decent survival mechanism for some species. One habit, given B⊗B's present state of anxious tiredness, is becoming problematic. His Spiritus intake. Though a long-term daily doser, his consumption pre-encounter was tempered, even modest. Since that critical moment, a stinging feeling of desperation often overpowers his restlessness as he lies awake in his anechoic crib. On many afternoons, his unease prompts him to slip unto to the Path to lick himself to a dumb stupor. This is a dubious strategy as the POMOC is more peopled during these hours and his way back to the Hole is hampered by a stumbling, inebriated gait. Intoxication as sleep inducer is an unreliable treatment method. Sometimes however, the volatile mix of untamable imagining and unnamable panic obliterates all good sensing. Impulsively, he will erupt in a fit of perilous behavior.

Outside, evening colored the light black. B⊗B stirred in Castle Keep. Having dined on a family of termites unwisely camped in the main passageway of his palace, he managed to steal a few sleep cycles, dreaming yet again of the house with the curtains and the cushy pillows and the hole in the ceiling through which the tremendous draft of outer forces swept him from his hands and feet in the whirling bliss of a palpable unknown. As he dozed he heard a sounding from his gut, from a resonant body-space gouged deep beneath the taut vibrations of his vocal folds.

SHIWA SHIWA TATT TATT GELUK ZIG HARA ZAG MARRO ING KWECK ING ZOION SUYA SUYA.

On cue, the familiar rhythms of the turbulent air crescendo in the emergence of the inevitable tidal wave hovering above his head. With ambiguous purpose it is at once the foreboding jaw of devouring hunger and the consuming comfort of a safeplace. *Zappaan!* He's never fearful when inside this recurring image yet it often wakes him with a feeling of irresolution.

Because it's so infrequent now, he takes his dreaming seriously. He apprehends more than usual these days as the folding convolutions of his waking and stuttering sleeping life produce uncanny nuance. The sensational top floor of his baroque dreamhouse reverberates in his lair. Multiple realities feed on each other in a masterly kneading movement. How many holes inhabit this topology he wonders? Two is already too much.

His thoughts divert momentarily to his favorite eating spot outside, The Scentuous Bakery. He feels hungry as he frivolously counts nine openings: mouth, anus, eyes, ears, nostrils, urethra, but only three present a credible thoroughfare of in and out. He's hypersensitive to this as all rats – field, lab, and city – have an innate orientation for entrance, exit, and escape holes. Speculation tends to intensify his hunger. Scraps of the holey bagel on his mind, he decides on the bakery kitchen for his first meal.

A walk-in establishment without the usual array of tables and upholstered chairs, the comings and goings here are quick and efficient. Crusty and baked doughmeat are amply littered beneath the main counter. In the kitchen area, raw flour, always a treat, is plentiful. He long ago plotted the optimal hours of invasion of this place. The baker's trade suits the normal rhythm of his existence. With the help of siblings, a hole has been carved in a room behind the kitchen where the food supplies are kept. It's easy prey if a rat knows to avoid the ridiculous traps placed in obvious nooks.

His health restored, B⊗B whets a now voracious appetite on the prospect of midnight breakfast. It feels so good to crave Upper World food again. The strangling encounter on the Path had caused his salivary gland to malfunction among other complications. Besides an incessantly dry mouth and difficulties swallowing, his desire for tasty bits evaporated. It provoked him to wonder in his endless awake moments whether salivating made him hungry or hunger made him salivate? It was a chicken and egg question he supposed. An ontological puzzle that kept him from feeling sorry for himself.

All organs and appendages working properly again, he breaks through the loose mortar hole in the kitchen's west wing.

23

Bette B's Affinities

Night 385

Night 388

*They operated on my ears last week replacing my cochlea with
artificial implants. I have tin ears now. I hear only a monotone
buzz, a bland, uninteresting narrow bandwidth noise. Something went wrong. They informed me of the unfortunate misstep
on a scrap of paper in doctor's scrawl. It said something like:
"The cochlear implants were successfully [unreadable]. How-*

ever, there is a mechanical problem with the device. We hope to solve it."

Night 390

ShazDada is certainly persistent. I agreed to give her a audio statement for her podcast.

Night 391

Thankfully I can still smell. They're less hasty to tamper with this sense since the implant failure. The new otolaryngologist (they replaced the other guy with someone more sympathetic to the clinic director's goals) is planning a radical laser surgery later this month. He writes me it will reduce my olfactory abilities by half. He tries to convince me that this procedure is good thing. He draws an anatomical picture of a rat's nose on a tablet to demonstrate what and where he will cauterize.

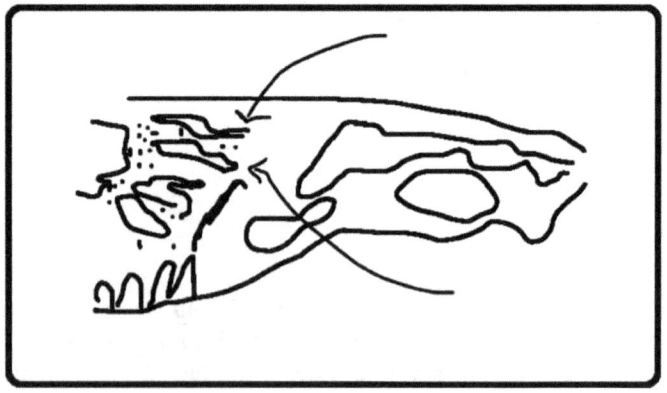

Night 393

I'm depressed, abject, blue, drowning. I wait. Wait for a blessed hemorrhage, for heart failure, a stroke. For a misplaced scalpel. For an unchecked morphine drip. For a stretch of rope.

Night 397

I have recorded my statement for Shaz. It came to me in a dream, emblazoned on the protest placard of a May '68 demonstrator on a sunny Parisian afternoon amid tufts of tear gas and burning cars. It goes like this:

It was there a horse soon dancing

24

Dust

B⊗B was busy. Much time had passed since he'd enjoyed supping in a world of tasty powders. Piles of pulverized grains and other foodstuffs were profusely scattered in this place. A hungry rat could choose from white, brown, and multi-grain flour. The sticky doughy bits of not-yet cupcakes and the crusty crumbs of croissant scraps were his favorites. He had an urge to embed his snout in the hole of a sesame bagel today, fastidiously gnawing away at its deliciousness from the inside out, emulating the style of a black hole consuming its event horizon. A tactical mating impulse to be sure, this eating inversion would enhance his pleasure of the meal.

Certainly desire in its many guises, drew him here. Down the slinky compressed dirt tunnel of the south-by-south-east common burrow and through the inconspicuous chip between the bricks behind the pastry oven. This was the entrance/exit for his species to another's source of daily bread. As usual, he made this journey alone. His solitary habits were beginning to irk him, to weigh on his innate sense of pack responsibility as well as his emotional want for company. His cousin's twice-monthly presence assuaged a minimum requirement of sociability but if he's honest with himself, it's not enough. It doesn't mend his self-imposed rupture with his fellows, his sensate requirement of belonging.

Agitated and disconcerted by unhappy feelings of solitude and social gaffery he devoured a quarter bag of sesame seeds, several walnuts, and a pecan. Finding residue from clover honey drippings on the floor near the marble pastry table he licked the stuff, careful not to bind his nails in its sticky mass.

Filled to bloating, BOB retreated to a dark corner near enough to the hole in the mortar to feel safe in a long respite of digestion. Satiated, the urge to exercise his laryngeal unit in this place of granulated particulates surprises him as he has not yet had his Spiritus fix. Can he sing un-soused? Worth a try he reckons as he deep breathes to prime his lungs for the test. He then emits a quavering 38 kHz tone, beautiful in its articulate simplicity. Expertly modulating his volume the slow rise and fall of this single unadorned pitch rides the drafty air inside and outside the kitchen like a wind swept plastic bag. Wafting. Delicate. Sonically available to a multitude of species and inorganic objects, he hopes it's soothing as he readies his folds for a more complex task.

Lately, he's been exercising his post-traumatic vocal artifacts to great effect. He's effortlessly acquired the magic ability to sound two pitches simultaneously, occasionally three. His control of frequency and resonation is still amateur but the trick itself is remarkable. This cooking space provides an ideal isolated rehearsal situation. Garnering his energies, he improvises, listening to the soundings that issue from his mouth with total concentration. He hits stride; is in a seamless reflexive mode of spontaneous precision. Each pitch massages the other as they interleave and separate, whispering and screaming, droning and shrilling. Immodestly it occurs to him he is producing tonalities of sonorous cacophony; the darkest darks and brightest brights. Remembering the sesame bagel he considers "Black Holey" as a potential band name if he and his cousin ever go public. He quickly reconsiders, deciding it's become a too trendy metaphor lately and he hates metaphors. He'll need to be more original. "Dust" maybe. Or "Dust Breeders." Keep it short, sweet, and existentially loaded. Generative matter and anti-matter. Mind-dust, magic dust, stardust. "Caught in the devil's bargain" dust to dust. Cool. He'll try the idea out on his cousin and anyway, he's ready to push his hospitality envelope a bit further. Dare to expose. Dare to share. Dare to collaborate ...

Engrossed in his own engagement, at first B⊗B took little notice of the effects his resonations were having on the objects nearby. Ceramic bowls were cracking at the strain of maintaining their form within this whirling crux of vibratory forces. Glass jars shattered, pouring their contents. When he sustained a fluctuating frequency of 38.5 kHz for over 10 seconds, metal spoons bent at the fulcrum of their handles and the marble tops of the pastry tables ripped fault lines. So resonant were his voicings that they incorporated the many layers of ongoing audial activity in the immediate environment. The pings, pangs, and pops were a chorus to his soaring solo. As in any full-functioning umwelt, the sonic signatures intertwined, knotted, reciprocated. In one brief ecstatic occurrence he felt a bodybuzz unlike anything produced by the taint of Spiritus.

The addition of the sinister, low-pitched growling sound percolating from the north corner of the kitchen convolved with the crackles and snaps, working well in the indeterminate composition. Is this what is meant by "sublime" B⊗B wondered as the kitchen deterritorialized around him? Or is it rather an act of "sublimation" as the alertness of his wide-awake processing wrapped itself in the somni-topos of his recurring dreamscape. He felt again the feeling of ascension to the upper floor of his illusory cushy house, folded in the embrace of variegated textures, riding wave upon wave in undulating anticipation.

He knew the freeze frame would soon follow. He waited for it. The beautiful overhanging arch of white-tipped blue blue blue, the humungous gaping jaw of the tsunami wave. He'd encountered this phantom so many times before ... and then ... again ... rising above his swooning body in suspended animation ... the enormous, pinkish, toothy, salivating jaw ...

25

Billy in the Box

Billy, the Bull Terrier pup in a box, was able to hear as most dogs do. His set of fur-frayed, rat-bitten ears may have looked stupid but they functioned impeccably. Wheeled around in the wee hours of a still vibrant city, he'd accustomed himself to nightlife, even if his handlers found the routine difficult. Usually he stayed caged in his cardboard doghouse, fitted with a flea infested blanket of some synthetic material or other, folded three times to provide a semblance of padding for his crumpled haunches. It was a relatively lazy life. He didn't at all miss the quotidian hunt. He had never really enjoyed the taste of rat flesh, finding it frankly unbearable to digest. He hated puking furballs. He was not a cat after all but a dog's dog. Though his species had been bred for this line of work, blood lunches weren't his thing. He preferred to hibernate and watch the world go by through the peephole Betty had punched out for him, perfectly framed by the capital "O" in "STORAGE" that was printed on his box.

On occasion, his genetic design would get the better of his docile personality. Rage of an uncontrollable nature would upset his calm. This temperament was often unleashed by sonic agitation. 38 kHz, a frequency outside human hearing, would trigger a sympathetic vibration in his dogbrain with painful results, just as the scent of

Rattus norvegicus could likely send him into a pre-programmed frenzy. The blue ones relied on this tendency of his for their own survival. He counted on it for exercise and satisfying a chromosomal desire to fulfill a mortal destiny. Nursing a strong allegiance to fated causality, he was an unapologetic "everything has a reason" advocate. It helped him remain placid when not on the hunt.

Betty and Bob often spoke about the GenTel's with derision, even as they lavished their pet with praise when he'd dutifully shake, gouge, or frighten a sewer rat to death, putting chicken wings on their aluminum camping plates and pummeled horsemeat in his bowl. Apparently it hadn't occurred to B & B that Billy was a precursor of genetic modification, a designer breed, a freaky Darwinian masterpiece. Billy didn't care one way or the other. Life was life and then it would be something else and he could barely contain his enthusiasm for that inevitability.

This late evening, or early morning, the Tuareg tribe of the POMOC domain had parked their household near The Scentuous Bakery to be first in line to grab fresh handouts of yeasty doughware ritually offered by the still sleepy bakers to the homeless, the nomads and the **PC**'s in this sprawling layer of goings on. Billy's temper raged to a flaming blue heat as a noise like no other split his eardrums, threatening the implosion of his every internal organ. Contorted by the persistent dissonant modulations that pierced his head and entrails, he barked, bounced, and rammed the sides of his box until Bob, slowly rising to his heavily booted feet, responded to the unnerving racket. Leaping from the confines of his perpendicular dog home, Billy was now unleashed to investigate the source of the problem.

Afterword

Belief, as "ultimate fact" of experience, is in the world's continued ability to surprise [...] Altogether, now:

The sense-awareness of the blue as situated in a certain event which I call the situation, is thus exhibited as the sense-awareness of a relation between the blue, the percipient event of the observer, the situation, and intervening events. All nature is in fact required.

Brian Massumi, *Too Blue*

And so I fell in love with a color — in this case, the color blue — as if falling under a spell, a spell I fought to stay under and get out from under, in turns.

Maggie Nelson, *Bluets*

Figures